AF584316

FLORA

AUSTRALIA'S MOST CURIOUS PLANTS

FLORA

AUSTRALIA'S MOST CURIOUS PLANTS

COMPANION BOOK TO FAUNA: AUSTRALIA'S MOST CURIOUS CREATURES

TANIA McCARTNEY

When it comes to flora, Australia is a land of diversity. From rainforests and deserts, to mountains and the seashore, 90 per cent of our plant life is unique to this ancient land. Treasures like our wattles, eucalypts, grass trees and banksias are part of our heritage and identity—and they still flourish here today, on the oldest landmass on Earth.

First Nations people have skilfully managed our native flora for over 65,000 years. Harnessing the power of plants for survival and culture, they continue to care for and hold a deep connection to our land. With over 1400 plant species under threat, protecting our plant life and learning land management from First Nations people is more vital than ever.

Australia has around 24,000 native plant species, which have adapted in pretty radical ways to our unique, dry land, including the use of fire and smoke in order to reproduce! FLORA explores just a small patch of these astonishing plants. From green giants to miniscule marvels, you'll learn how plants grow, how they are used by humans and other animals, and how strange, life-giving yet deadly they can be. Most importantly, you'll learn how vital plants are for our country's biodiversity, for healthy ecosystems—and for the future of our planet.

There are a lot of peculiar and cool scientific words in FLORA. Discover their meaning in the glossary at the end of the book. Conservation status also appears alongside many plants.

LET'S EXPLORE OUR CURIOUS PLANTS!

BINOMIAL NAMES

As you move through FLORA, you'll notice names (in brackets) for each plant. These are scientific classifications—or binomial names—and are always written in *italics*. For example, the golden wattle has the binomial name *Acacia pycnantha*. The first word is the plant's genus (the plural of genus is 'genera') and the second word is its species. You may sometimes see an abbreviation like *A. pycnantha*. This is just a shorter way to write the name of each species. If you see 'spp.' after a genus name—*Acacia* spp.—this refers to more than one species in the genus *Acacia* (our yellow puffball wattles).

CONTENTS

CONSERVATION STATUS

- EX EXTINCT
- EW EXTINCT IN THE WILD
- CR CRITICALLY ENDANGERED
- EN ENDANGERED
- VU VULNERABLE
- NT NEAR THREATENED
- CD CONSERVATION DEPENDENT*
- LC LEAST CONCERN

*Conservation dependent means plants rely on a conservation program for their survival.

FLORA LANDSCAPES

Australia is the flattest, lowest and driest of all inhabited continents on Earth, yet our ancient land bustles with unique and rather curious native flora. This is thanks to our isolation from the rest of the world, and the remarkable ways our plants have adapted to survive. Our great southern land is divided into climate zones and a range of landscapes and habitats where local flora thrives.

DESERT

Australia is dry. Around 35 per cent of our mainland is classified as desert and a whopping 70 per cent is considered 'desert-like'. Plant life includes shrubs, trees, spinifex and other grasses. Water-hogging succulents and vivid wildflowers abound in some regions.

OUR COMBINED DESERTS COVER 2.7 MILLION KM^2

HARD SPINIFEX (*Triodia* spp.)

RIVERS AND LAKES

Along with our many lakes and wetlands, our rivers teem with plant life, from saltbush and mulga to reeds and algae. Our largest lake, Kati Thanda–Lake Eyre, spends most of its time completely dry, yet when rains do come, plants pop with a watercolour wash of colour.

SACRED LOTUS (*Nelumbo nucifera*)

CLIMATE ZONES

Our main plant regions are rainforest, sclerophyll forest (eucalypts), woodland, grassland and savanna. Each of these regions straddles four major climate zones that influence the kind of flora that grows there.

TROPICAL

Deciduous trees, grasses, mangroves and jungle-like rainforest species.

ARID

Grasses, mallee trees, hummock grass, shrubs, grass trees and wildflowers.

TEMPERATE

Wet sclerophyll forest trees, woodland trees, grass, scrub and temperate rainforest species.

COOL

Sclerophyll woodland trees, eucalypt forests, temperate rainforest trees and alpine plants.

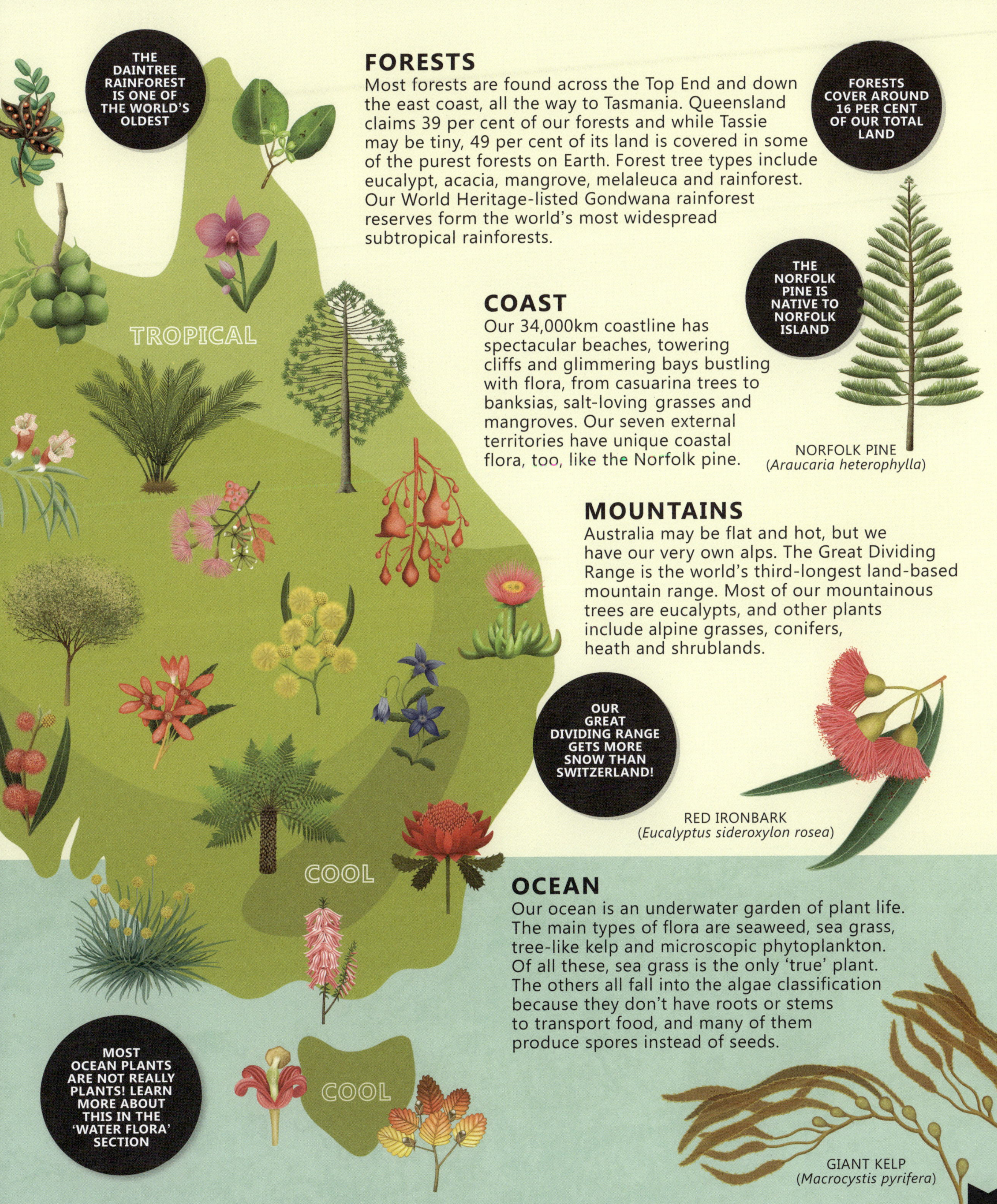

FORESTS

Most forests are found across the Top End and down the east coast, all the way to Tasmania. Queensland claims 39 per cent of our forests and while Tassie may be tiny, 49 per cent of its land is covered in some of the purest forests on Earth. Forest tree types include eucalypt, acacia, mangrove, melaleuca and rainforest. Our World Heritage-listed Gondwana rainforest reserves form the world's most widespread subtropical rainforests.

COAST

Our 34,000km coastline has spectacular beaches, towering cliffs and glimmering bays bustling with flora, from casuarina trees to banksias, salt-loving grasses and mangroves. Our seven external territories have unique coastal flora, too, like the Norfolk pine.

NORFOLK PINE
(*Araucaria heterophylla*)

MOUNTAINS

Australia may be flat and hot, but we have our very own alps. The Great Dividing Range is the world's third-longest land-based mountain range. Most of our mountainous trees are eucalypts, and other plants include alpine grasses, conifers, heath and shrublands.

RED IRONBARK
(*Eucalyptus sideroxylon rosea*)

OCEAN

Our ocean is an underwater garden of plant life. The main types of flora are seaweed, sea grass, tree-like kelp and microscopic phytoplankton. Of all these, sea grass is the only 'true' plant. The others all fall into the algae classification because they don't have roots or stems to transport food, and many of them produce spores instead of seeds.

GIANT KELP
(*Macrocystis pyrifera*)

PARTS OF A PLANT

Plants are jaw-dropping. Thousands of one-celled phytoplankton can be found in a single teaspoon of ocean water, yet our tallest tree—a mountain ash (*Eucalyptus regnans*) in Tasmania —is as high as a 30-storey building (100m)! Our flora is built in a variety of ways, but over 90 per cent share some kind of roots, stems, leaves, flowers, fruits and seeds.

ROOTS

Roots are a plant's anchor. They absorb and store food and water. Most plants have a short, thick tap root from which smaller roots grow, and many have hairy, fibrous roots with a large surface area to suck in water and nutrients. Other types of root include aerial, buttress, stilt and pneumatophore—which act like snorkels so that waterlogged mangroves can 'breathe' oxygen.

ROOTS MAKE GROWTH HORMONES SO NEW PLANTS CAN MAGICALLY SPRING FROM ROOTS, STEMS OR LEAVES! THIS IS CALLED VEGETATIVE REPRODUCTION

STEMS

Stems are the plant's spine. They sprout all-important leaves and transport water and nutrients from root to leaf and back again. Most stems grow above ground but some grow underground, like rhizomes, corms, bulbs and tubers. The everyday potato and the bush food yam daisy (*Microseris lanceolata)* are called 'root' veggies but they are really modified underground stems!

TRUNKS AND BRANCHES ARE REALLY JUST WOODY STEMS COVERED IN LAYERS OF BARK

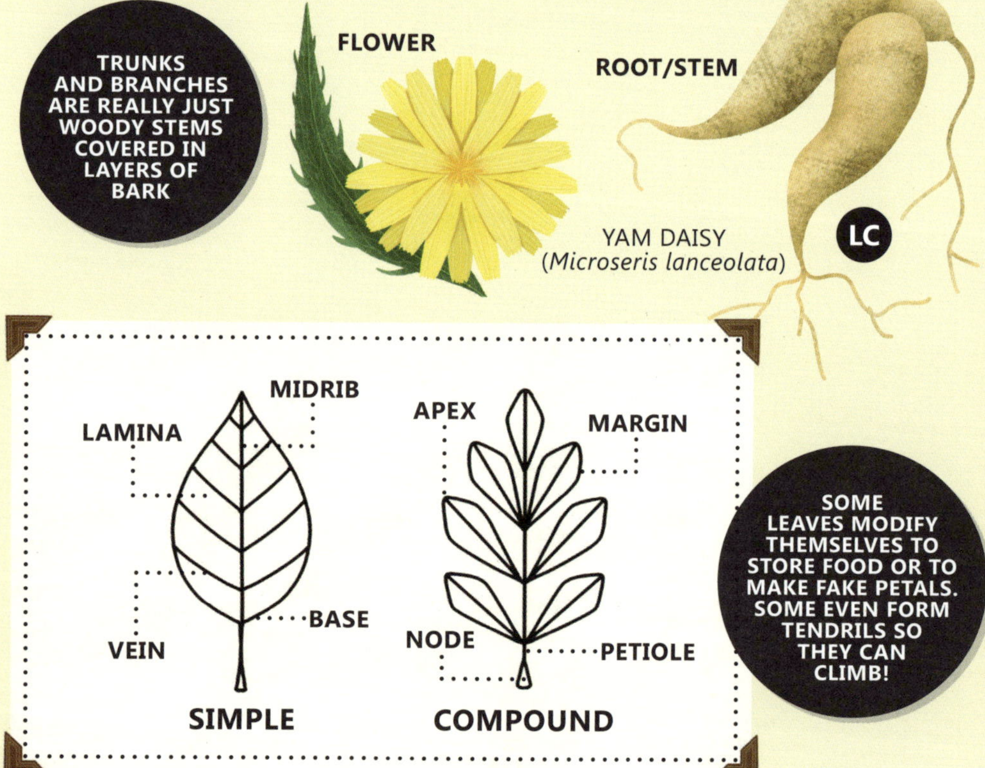

YAM DAISY (*Microseris lanceolata*)

SOME LEAVES MODIFY THEMSELVES TO STORE FOOD OR TO MAKE FAKE PETALS. SOME EVEN FORM TENDRILS SO THEY CAN CLIMB!

LEAVES

Leaves are the feeders. They have three main parts—the base, the petiole (stem) and the lamina (blade). The apex is the tip and the margin is the outer edge. Simple leaves have one leaf blade while compound leaves have many blades, called leaflets. The little bump where a leaf grows from a stalk is called a node.

INFLORESCENCE

Many Australian flowers, like the coastal banksia, are not single flowers at all. They are a group of tiny blooms or specially modified leaves (bracts) that form a bunch or a 'flower head'. The scientific name for this kind of flower is an 'inflorescence'.

COASTAL BANKSIA (*Banksia integrifolia*)

LC

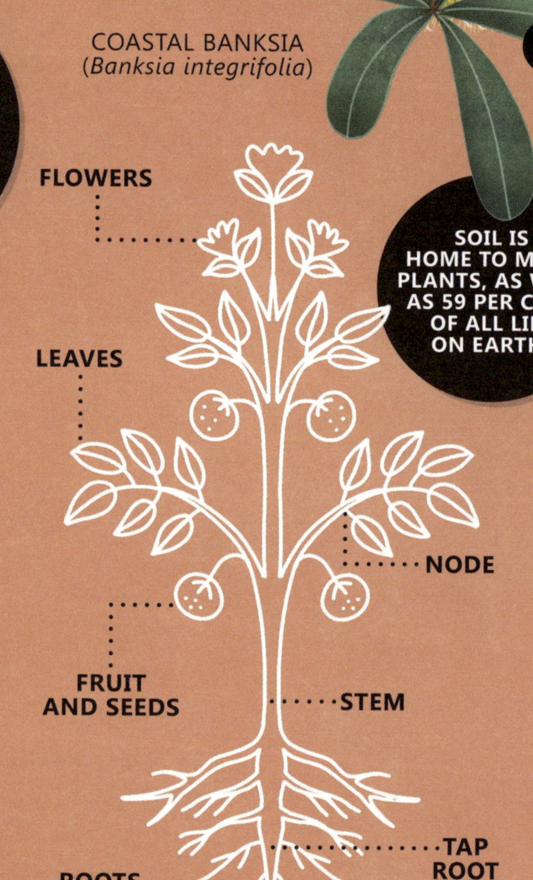

SOIL IS HOME TO MOST PLANTS, AS WELL AS 59 PER CENT OF ALL LIFE ON EARTH!

THE RACE TO THE SUN

Around 450 million years ago, plants grew to new heights (literally). Vascular plants emerged, with long stems to help them reach more sunlight and get much better at photosynthesis. There are two types of tissue running through vascular stems. Xylem tissue carries water and nutrients up from the roots and phloem tissue carries sugars produced by the leaves. Non-vascular plants (like moss and algae) don't have this tissue. They just pass nutrients from one cell to another.

VASCULAR PLANTS MAKE UP 90 PER CENT OF ALL FLORA

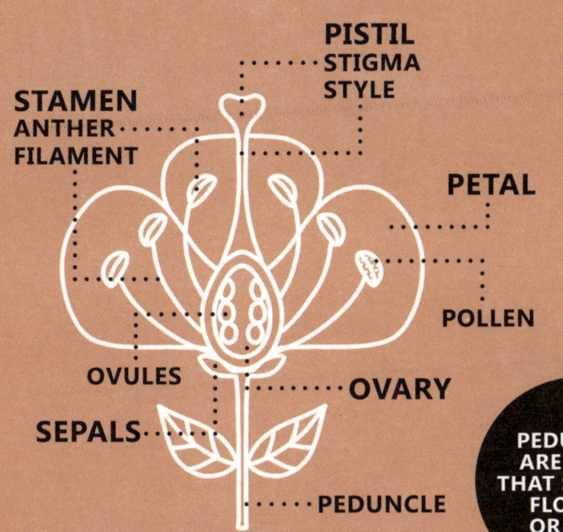

PEDUNCLES ARE STEMS THAT SUPPORT FLOWERS OR FRUIT

LOVE IS IN THE AIR

When animals carry pollen to flowers, the pollen catches on the stigma then travels down the style to the ovary. Hey presto! The flower is fertilised.

FEMALE BULOKE CONE
(*Allocasuarina luehmannii*)

CONES NOT FRUITS

Gymnosperms, like conifers and ferns, have cones (not fruits), and cones are pollinated by spores (not pollen). Spores are carried on the wind from male cones to female cones. When the fertilised female cones dry out and crack open, the seeds and their papery wings catch on the wind and fly away to start life anew.

FLOWERS

Flowers are the show-offs—they use colour and scent to attract pollinators. These beauties have five main parts.

- **STAMEN** Male part with filaments, plus anthers that make pollen.
- **PISTIL** Female part with a long tube (style) that leads down to the flower's ovary. At the top is a sticky stigma that collects pollen.
- **OVARY** Female part with ovules that become seeds after fertilisation.
- **PETALS** Rather glamorous and perhaps even fragrant leaves!
- **SEPALS** Leaves that enclose flower buds till they bloom, then stick around to provide support at the base of the flower.

KAKADU PLUM
(*Terminalia ferdinandiana*)

FRUITS

Fruits are growth chambers. They are actually ripened ovaries with little ovules that become seeds. Some fruits don't need to be fertilised, and these are called parthenocarpic fruit. A plant's growth hormones will help them mature and the adult plant grows fruit with no seeds at all—like seedless watermelon.

SEEDS

Seeds are new life. When they detect warmth and moisture, it's time to germinate. Seeds have three main parts. The seed coat protects the seed, the endosperm has nutrients for growth and the cotyledons are baby leaves that pop out and poke through the soil.

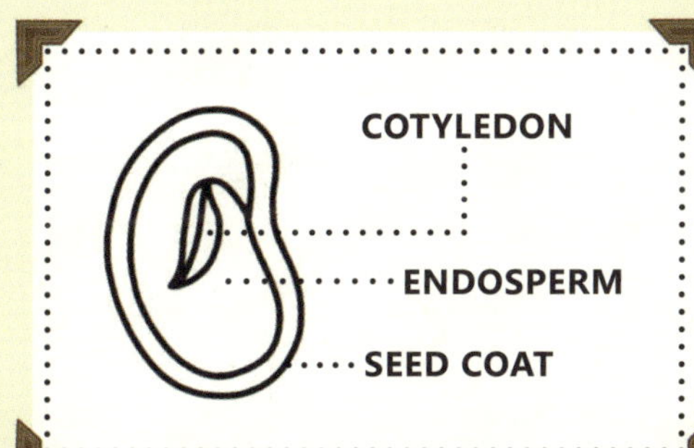

PHOTOSYNTHESIS RECIPE

How do plants eat? True masterchefs, they use a very special recipe.

INGREDIENTS

- Water
- Sunlight
- Carbon dioxide (CO_2)

DIRECTIONS

- **STEP 1** Leaves soak up sunlight with cells called chloroplasts that act like tiny solar panels. At the same time, roots suck up water.
- **STEP 2** The CO_2 you breathe out every day is 'breathed in' through tiny holes (called stomata) in the plant's leaves.
- **STEP 3** Inside the plant's tiny solar panels, a green pigment called chlorophyll uses sunlight to turn water and CO_2 into a delicious type of sugar called glucose (lunch).
- **STEP 4** The plants gobble this glucose to grow big and strong, and as they do this, they 'breathe out' oxygen. Bon appétit!

EUCALYPTS

The tallest flowering plants on earth, eucalypt trees (also called gum trees) are the dominators—making up over three-quarters of Australia's native forest area. They are from the Eucalypteae tribe of the myrtle (Myrtaceae) family, which includes species in three genera—*Angophora*, *Corymbia* and *Eucalyptus*. There are around 800 species of eucalypt, and almost all are endemic to our shores (found nowhere else!).

GREAT SURVIVORS

Eucalypts evolved from rainforest ancestors and cleverly adapted to some pretty dry, rugged land, with poor soil quality. Over millions of years, they developed cool survival strategies against fire, drought or just plain hard living:

- **EPICORMIC BUDS** hide under bark and sprout new leaves once fire has passed.
- **LIGNOTUBER BULBS** at the base of trunks contain buds and food for resprouting.
- **COPPICING** is when a tree grows new shoots from a cut stump or even a root.
- **SELF-PRUNING** is when trees drop lower branches to remove fuel for fire.

LIGNOTUBER

UNDER GROUND

LIGNOTUBERS CAN SURVIVE MANY FIRES AND CAN LIVE FOR HUNDREDS OF YEARS

MONGARLOWE MALLEE

(*Eucalyptus recurva*)

The critically endangered Mongarlowe mallee, with its unique curling leaves, is Australia's loneliest tree. Discovered in 1985 near Braidwood, NSW, only six trees remain and two of them could be over 13,000 years old, making them the oldest trees on Earth!

THIS MALLEE IS ALSO KNOWN AS THE ICE AGE GUM

CR

SUGAR GLIDER
(*Petaurus breviceps*)

GUM TREES

Inspired by the Sydney red gum (*Angophora costata*), English botanist Sir Joseph Banks called eucalypts gum trees because of their sticky, gummy red sap. Sugar gliders love this sap. They eagerly dig into the tree's bark to feast on nature's candy.

HIGH AND LOW

Both the largest and smallest eucalypts live in Tasmania. The giant mountain ash (*E. regnans*) can grow as high as 100m yet the varnished gum (*E. vernicosa*) shrub grows to just 50cm.

I. *E. regnans* II. *E. camaldulensis* III. *E. leucoxylon*
IV. *E. caesia* V. *Homo sapiens* VI. *E. vernicosa*

USEFUL FLORA

Used for construction, fuel, oil, furniture and more, eucalypts can reach 37m in just three years, making them a sustainable source of wood. First Nations people have used eucalypts for countless purposes, including musical instruments, canoes, insect repellents, medicines, and for cultural ceremonies, too.

THIS RED GUM'S FLOWERS HAVE FEWER STAMENS, GIVING THEM A UNIQUE LOOK

NEW KID

The *Corymbia* genus is a new classification. Trees like the red-flowering gum (*Corymbia ficifolia*) were given their own genus in the early 1990s because of the way they differ from 'true' eucalypts. As botanists learn more about our flora, new classifications emerge all the time.

LC

RED-FLOWERING GUM
(*Corymbia ficifolia*)

SCRIBBLY MOTH
(*Ogmograptis scribula*)

SCRIBBLY GUM

(*E. haemastoma*)

The scribbly gum hosts an annual bark show, with works by some curious local artists—the larvae of the scribbly moth. These larvae tunnel their way beneath the top layer of bark, and when summer comes and the tree's bark is shed, artistic trails are revealed. This gum and its artworks can be found in the *Snugglepot and Cuddlepie* books by May Gibbs, where the characters call these scribbles 'fairy writing'.

ALMOST ALL CRITICALLY ENDANGERED LEADBEATER'S POSSUMS LIVE IN VICTORIA'S MOUNTAIN ASH FORESTS

RIVER RED GUM

(*E. camaldulensis*)

The river red gum is the most widely distributed of all eucalypts. It can survive in flood waters thanks to special tissue (aerenchyma) that forms air pockets so oxygen can reach underwater roots. This gum has—you guessed it—bright red timber and is one of our eucalypt jumbos, measuring 5m around the trunk and 45m high.

TIMBER

NT

BINYAL BIRTHING TREES

FIRE AND TERMITES OFTEN HOLLOW OUT THE HUGE TRUNKS OF BINYAL (RIVER RED GUM) TREES. THE WIRADJURI PEOPLE USED THE HOLLOWS AS SAFE PLACES TO REST OR FOR MOTHERS TO GIVE BIRTH. BEFORE USING THE HOLLOWS, THEY WOULD SMOKE OUT UNWANTED SPIDERS AND SNAKES, AS WELL AS BUSH FOOD LIKE POSSUMS.

GREENGROCER CICADA
(*Cyclochila australasiae*)

LC BLOSSOM

LEAF

TASMANIAN MOUNTAIN ASH

(*E. regnans*)

Exclusive to Tasmania and a few areas in southern Victoria, our native giant grows more than a metre each year and can live around 400 years. 'Centurion'—a whopper in Tasmania—holds the world record as both the tallest flowering plant and the tallest hardwood tree!

100m

FRIENDLY FAUNA

Birds and bees adore eucalypt nectar, and greengrocer cicada babies suck sap from eucalypt roots for as long as seven years! During the daytime, lesser long-eared bats hide in tree cracks and hollow limbs, and then there's the koala, whose survival is totally dependent on these trees.

LEAVES, GUMNUTS, BLOSSOMS

Eucalypts may be tall, hardy and impressive—but it's the up-close, finer details that are truly intriguing.

TYPES OF BLOSSOM

Eucalypt blossoms come in many colours and can be small, sweet and single or large, showy and clustered. They are made up of stacks of stamens that grow under a little cap called an operculum. As the flower matures, the cap eases off, and the stamens pop out. Why so many stamens? The more the better for pollination. Plus, they look pretty—and pollinators love pretty. Here are some of the most common blossom structures:

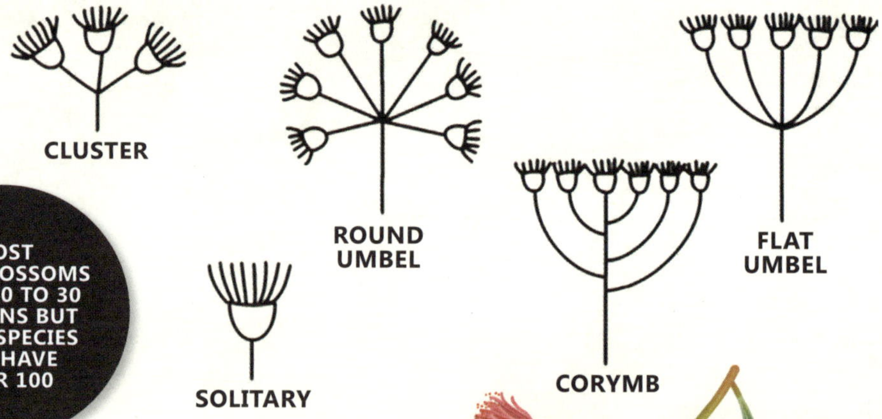

CLUSTER

ROUND UMBEL

FLAT UMBEL

SOLITARY

CORYMB

MOST GUM BLOSSOMS HAVE 20 TO 30 STAMENS BUT SOME SPECIES CAN HAVE OVER 100

IF YOU'RE EVER LOST IN THE BUSH WITHOUT WATER, A LITRE OR MORE CAN BE TAPPED FROM THE ROOTS OF THE LERP MALLEE

LC

LERP MALLEE
(*E. incrassata*)

THICK AND LIGHT IN COLOUR, RED IRONBARK HONEY HAS A HINT OF ALMONDS

HONEY TIME

Eucalypts make a lot of nectar and are a bee-favourite. Famous Aussie eucalypt honeys include yellow box, ironbark and blue gum. They're not only delicious and nutritious—they can last forever. Pots of 3000-year-old honey were once found in ancient Egypt—and the honey was still good!

60,000 BEES MUST VISIT OVER TWO MILLION FLOWERS TO GATHER ENOUGH NECTAR FOR JUST ONE JAR OF HONEY

FLORA HONEY
Ironbark
NET WT 450g

LC

RED IRONBARK
(*E. sideroxylon rosea*)

TYPES OF BARK

A eucalypt's bark forms a protective layer that dies off each year, usually in summer. There are many types, from thick, spongy strands to popcorn-like knobbles. There's also crackled, flaky, patchy, ribbon-like and even furry-looking bark. These barks have a variety of descriptive names, but you could make up your own!

FIBROUS | GRANULAR | RIBBON | SMOOTH | TESSELLATED | MOTTLED

TOXIC LEAVES

Eucalypts are sclerophylls, which means 'hard-leaved'. To preserve water, their leaves are often thick and leathery, and hang straight downwards to avoid the midday sun. These leaves are packed with a toxic ingredient called cineole, which puts off hungry herbivores—though not the koala! In fact, only a few insects and three mammals can eat these leaves—the koala, the greater glider and the ring-tail possum. Each have specialised digestive tracts to deal with that nasty cineole.

LC ROUND-LEAVED MALLEE (*E. orbifolia*)

VU SILVER-LEAVED MOUNTAIN GUM (*E. pulverulenta*)

LC TASMANIAN BLUE GUM (*E. globulus*)

NT RIVER RED GUM (*E. camaldulensis*) with juvenile leaf

VU WILLOW PEPPERMINT (*E. nicholii*)

TYPES OF LEAF

Eucalypts have a wide range of leaf types, with most appearing long and narrow, broad or oval. Juvenile leaves can look very different. They are softer and more rounded while adult leaves are thicker and more oval (often with that real gumleaf curve).

EXPLOSIVE FRUIT

Gum blossoms have no petals—they are simply a cap of fluffy stamens. When the flowers die off, hard gumnuts develop, turning brown and woody. Some types of gumnut are so hard, they need fire to open them, and some don't just peel or pop open to release seeds—they explode!

EUREKA!

Eucalyptus tree roots delve deep, drawing up water, minerals and also metals from the soil. Any traces of nearby gold end up stored in the tree's leaves and can indicate stores of gold in the ground below. A Maia detector (X-ray) can reveal any gold in a tree's leaf, and this method is actually used for gold-hunting in the Kalgoorlie region of Western Australia. Treasure hunters rejoice!

ROSE OF THE WEST

(*Eucalyptus macrocarpa*)

The largest eucalypt blossom belongs to the rose of the west, with its octopus-arm branches that sprout from a lignotuber at the base of the plant. Its leaves are 'sessile', meaning they sit right on the stem, with no leaf stalk at all. Both their spectacular red blossoms and space ship-like gumnuts can measure 10cm wide!

ACACIA

Acacia (wattle) trees just love arid or semi-arid regions, yet are still found all over Australia. This makes them our most common tree after eucalypts. They are also our largest genus of flowering plants—we have around 1000 of the world's 1350 species. Wattles are actually a member of the pea family! This is why you'll find their seeds tucked inside pods, just like garden peas.

LEAVES

Wattles have lots of leaf types and many grow several types on the same plant. Their long, single leaves aren't leaves at all—they are flattened stalks called phyllodes. Seedlings do produce 'true' leaves, but these are later replaced by the phyllodes, which contain water-holding cells. 'True' wattle leaves are more fernlike—and the leaves of some species can actually move! They close to protect themselves from water loss and hungry wallabies, or even to avoid hot sun (called thigmonasty). Others close when the sun goes down and open when it comes up again (called nyctinasty).

WATTLES ONLY LIVE UP TO 40 YEARS YET SOME EUCALYPTS CAN LIVE 1000 YEARS

GOLDEN WATTLE (*A. pycnantha*)

A SWEET OIL CALLED 'MIMOSA' COMES FROM CERTAIN ACACIAS AND ITS AROMA CAN CALM NOISY CHILDREN!

ACACIAS ARE FOUND ALL OVER AUSTRALIA

GOLDEN WATTLE

(*Acacia pycnantha*)

Like all acacias, golden wattle handles dry regions and drought with ease. When this wattle's pods mature, they split open and spill their delicious seeds. Wattleseeds are a popular bush food and the seeds of this species have a coffee vanilla flavour. The golden wattle is Australia's national floral emblem because, like Australians, it's found in every state and territory.

WATTLES ARE ONE OF THE FIRST PLANTS TO FLOURISH AFTER BUSHFIRES AND ONE OF THE FIRST TO BLOOM AHEAD OF SPRING

RHIZOBIA

NITROGEN FIXERS

The wattle's vast network of roots absorbs nitrogen from the air, 'fixes' (converts) it for plant use, then spreads it through the ground via its roots. Bacteria (called rhizobia) help the plant do this, and the result is fabulous for the soil and for other plants (and animals), too.

USEFUL FLORA

Acacia wood is fast-growing and very hard so it's perfect for fencing and buildings. Early settlers built wattle-and-daub huts by making frames with wattle branches daubed in mud. Acacias are also used for medicines, dyes, skincare and perfume. Wattle tree roots can be roasted and eaten!

SEEDS WITH ARILS

GREEN-HEAD ANT (*Rhytidoponera metallica*)

UNDERGROUND SEED OPS

Just like peas, wattles are a type of legume, so they grow pods for their seeds. Each seed has a fleshy attachment called an aril. When ants take seeds to their underground nests, they nibble at the aril, leaving the seeds untouched. These seeds can stay underground for many years, waiting patiently for the next rain.

BLOSSOMS

Wattle flowers are famously bright gold but a Queensland species has mauvey-pink flowers, a species from Western Australia has snowy white flowers and a Victorian variety's blossoms are cheeky red.

FRIENDLY FAUNA

Squirrel gliders and birds feast on acacia's sugary sap and nectar, or snap up insects attracted by its puffball blossoms. Many birds love its seeds, especially the honeyeater. Yellow-tailed black cockatoos rip the wattle's bark to find and devour juicy grubs.

GUBA BOOMERANGS

WIRADJURI PEOPLE HAVE ALWAYS PRIZED THE LONG-LASTING WOOD OF THE GUBA (COOBA WATTLE). THIS WOOD IS BRILLIANT FOR CRAFTING BOOMERANGS BECAUSE IT DOESN'T WARP OR TWIST.

RAINY DAYS

Also called the 'rain tree', some wattles fold up their leaves when the rains come. This clever trick means the water falls through to the soil below where it can be sucked up by thirsty roots.

FROM BUD TO BLOSSOM

POMPOM BLOOMS

The wattle's fuzzy pompom flower is actually a bunch of teensy flowers that form a ball (an inflorescence). Their floral, woody aroma is adored by bees—and the perfume industry!

STINKING WATTLE

(*Acacia cambagei*)

This poor wattle really stinks. Literally! The pong comes from the tree's bark and leaves, and some say it smells like sewerage, boiled cabbage—even old socks or the rotten breath of a camel! This tree has very hard wood that can burn for hours.

ACACIA HONEY HAS A DELICATE, FLORAL VANILLA FLAVOUR AND IT'S SO PALE, IT'S ALMOST TRANSPARENT

SHORT AND TALL

Smaller than eucalypts, acacia trees can reach up to 20m high—like the blackwood wattle (*A. melanoxylon*) yet acacia shrubs can be as small as 30cm—like the grass wattle (*A. willdenowiana*).

GRASS WATTLE
(*A. willdenowiana*)

PROTEACEAE

Australia split from the ancient landmass of Gondwana around 45 million years ago, and that's when this prehistoric family of flowering plants really took root. There are more than 1500 species of Proteaceae worldwide, with most—an impressive 860!—native to Australia. Our home-grown family includes some real stunners, like waratahs, grevilleas, banksias, hakeas and macadamias.

UNLIKE MOST FLOWERING PLANTS THAT BLOOM FROM SPRING THROUGH SUMMER, PROTEACEAE FLOWER FROM AUTUMN THROUGH WINTER AND INTO SPRING

SEED WARRIORS

The seed pods of some banksia species are sealed shut with resin. As part of a process called serotiny, the heat of fire melts the resin and the pods pop open to release their seeds. As these plants are often found in bad-quality soil, the rich ash layer left after a fire makes a perfect nursery for seeds.

HAIRPIN BANKSIA SEEDS (*Banksia spinulosa*)

FIRE! FIRE!

Great bushfire survivors, this family has thick trunks that resist heat damage. Once fire has passed, epicormic buds beneath the bark will pop out and the plant is magically reborn. Like eucalypt trees, many Proteaceae have lignotubers—swollen underground tubers at their base that can resprout after fire. Many species need fire to open their seed pods.

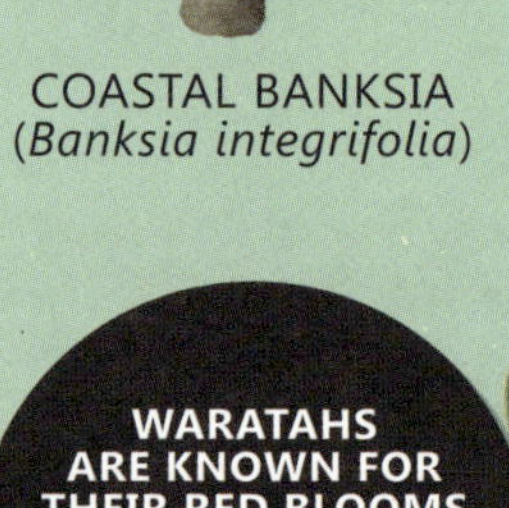

LC

COASTAL BANKSIA (*Banksia integrifolia*)

WARATAHS ARE KNOWN FOR THEIR RED BLOOMS BUT THEY ALSO COME IN YELLOW, PINK, WHITE AND PALEST GREEN

LC

SHADY LADY WHITE WARATAH (*Telopea speciosissima x oreades*)

INFLORESCENCE

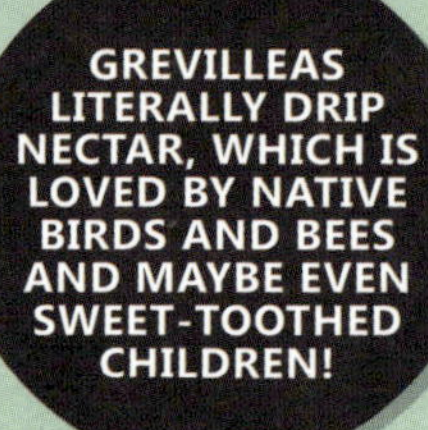

GREVILLEAS LITERALLY DRIP NECTAR, WHICH IS LOVED BY NATIVE BIRDS AND BEES AND MAYBE EVEN SWEET-TOOTHED CHILDREN!

LC

GREVILLEA ELEGANCE (*Grevillea longistyla x johnsonii*)

CAPER WHITE BUTTERFLY (*Belenois java*)

TRICKY BLOSSOMS

Proteaceae flowers aren't what they seem. Their striking blossoms might look like a single flower but they're either a mass of tiny buds or a large, cone-like head surrounded by hundreds (or even thousands) of teensy flowers. Both kinds are called a flower head or inflorescence.

PROTEACEAE LEAVES

The leaves of Proteaceae are super tough and sometimes hairy, with thick spines, needles, toxic chemicals and other defences. This family is also famous for its variety of leaves, sometimes with several types on the one plant.

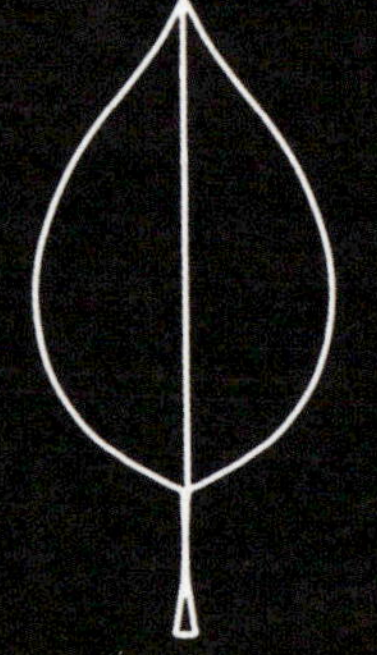

SIMPLE

COMPOUND

BIPINNATE

PALMATE

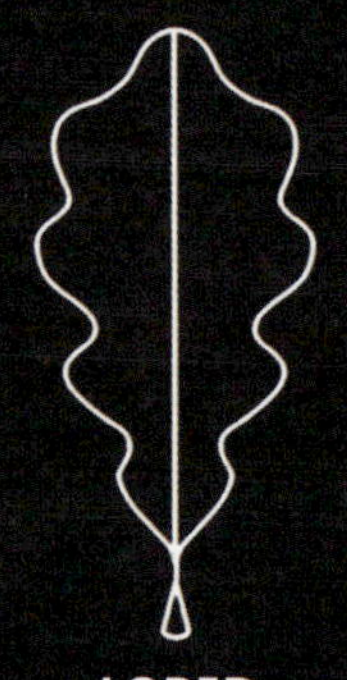

LOBED

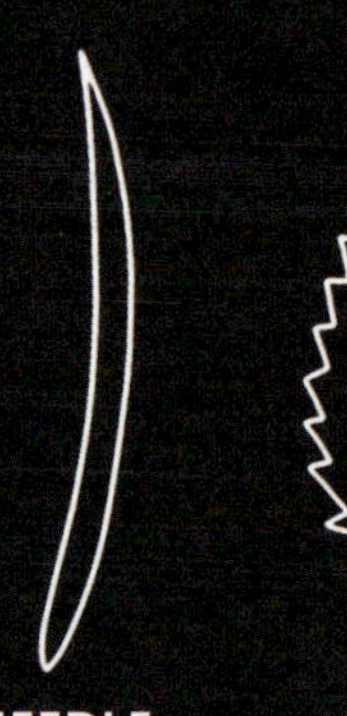

NEEDLE

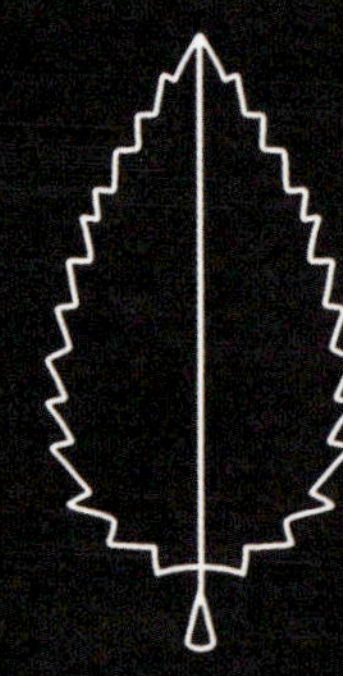

SERRATED

SMOOTH SHELL MACADAMIA

(Macadamia integrifolia)

Macadamia nuts are prized worldwide, and the smooth shell macadamia is the most popular species for nut production. Macadamia nuts (or seeds) have one of the hardest shells of all nuts. They're so hard to open, they need specialised tools ... or an elephant. Even then, an elephant would need to balance all its weight on a tennis ball to achieve the kind of force required to crack open this nut (300psi). The Bulburin nut (*Macadamia jansenii*) is one of our most endangered species, with just 90 trees remaining.

LC

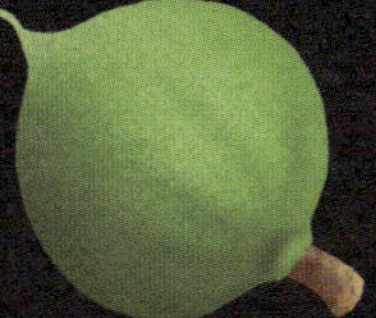

FRUIT

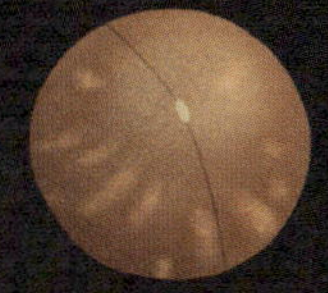

OPEN FRUIT

SHELL

OPEN SHELL

NUT (SEED)

HUNGRY ELEPHANT

GIANT CANDLES BANKSIA

(Banksia ericifolia x spinulosa)

The blooms of the giant candles banksia can grow up to 40cm long! This banksia is a hybrid, which is a blend of two or more plant species. When you see an 'x' in the binomial name, you know it's a hybrid.

WHEN YOU AND THE ELEPHANT DO MANAGE TO CRACK A MACADAMIA, BE SURE TO KEEP THE NUT AWAY FROM YOUR POOCH—THEY ARE TOXIC TO DOGS

OLD SMOKY

To trigger germination, some Proteaceae species have seeds that rely on chemical compounds found in smoke. When they 'smell' smoke, they get set to release their seed!

THE CANDLESTICK BANKSIA HAS CLEVER HYDROPHOBIC LEAVES THAT REPEL WATER, REDUCING ITS RISK OF FUNGAL DISEASE

LC

KING'S HOLLY

(Lomatia tasmanica)

Proteaceae species make up 20 per cent of our endangered and 19 per cent of our critically endangered plants. One critically endangered plant is Tasmania's king's holly, which is one of the world's oldest living plant species. It can't produce seeds, so the 500 remaining plants have self-cloned for the past 43,000 years!

BRUSH FIRE

THE NOONGAR-WUDJARI PEOPLE DRIED THE CONES OF THE WARRNINY (PROSTRATE BANKSIA) TO USE AS HAIR BRUSHES. THEY ALSO LIT THEM TO MAKE TORCHES OR JUST TO KEEP THEMSELVES WARM!

RISKY BUSINESS

Cloning is risky for plants because each clone carries the same DNA as the rest. This puts them at risk of catching a disease that could wipe out the entire population. Genetic diversity is important for survival.

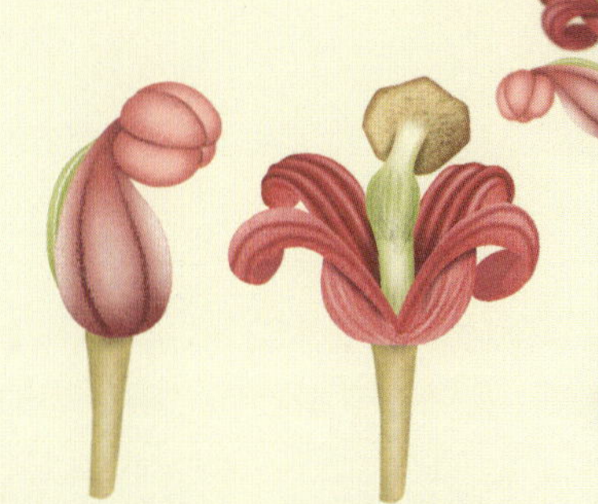

CLOSED BUD OPEN BUD

CR

FRIENDLY FAUNA

Proteaceae attract certain types of animals, including pygmy possums, which help with pollination and seed dispersal by eating (then pooping out) the seeds. Flower species with strong scents attract bees, beetles and ants, while species with no scent rely on large, showy flowers and fruit to attract birds and mammals.

BANDED SUGAR ANT
(Camponotus consobrinus)

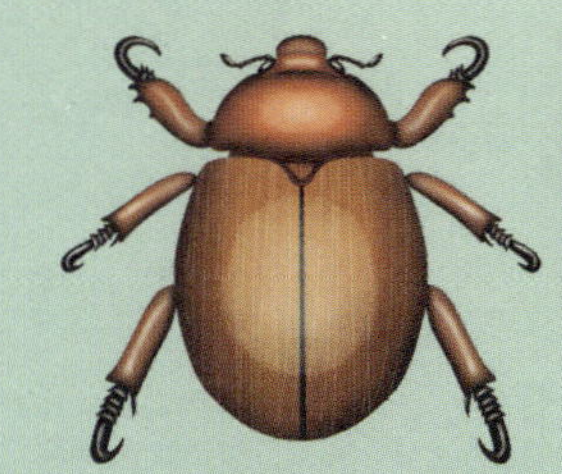

CHRISTMAS BEETLE
(Anoplognathus viriditarsis)

BIRDS, BEES AND BUTTERFLIES GET ALL THE POLLINATION CREDIT—BUT BEETLES, ANTS, LIZARDS, BATS AND MANY OTHER MAMMALS HELP OUT, TOO!

GONDWANA GARDEN

Australia was the last continent to break from Gondwana, and when we sailed away, our native plants hitched a ride. Rainforests covered much of Australia at the time, but as our continent drifted north (it's still drifting!), it became drier—turning into the open grasslands and deserts we know today.

BANKSIA

(*Banksia* spp.)

This iconic plant dates back more than 40 million years and all but one of the world's 173 species are native to Australia. Their flower cones are more like bunches of fruit! When flowers die off, their woody cones form hard seedpod fruits (called follicles) with one or two seeds inside. But of course, with our radical banksias, the follicles can only open with the help of blazing fire. Most banksias produce an overload of nectar (said to smell like fresh bread dough!) and some use this aroma to attract nocturnal animals for night pollination.

THE BANKSIA WAS NAMED AFTER BOTANIST SIR JOSEPH BANKS

LC

SHOWY BANKSIA (*Banksia speciosa*)

WARATAH

(*Telopea* spp.)

There are five species of waratah—all found on our east coast. Each flower is described as a cone and every 'petal' around the outside is a bract (modified leaf). The inner part of the flower is a mass of up to 240 tiny flowers, forming a stunning inflorescence, and as it has no fragrance, the plant relies on this bloom to attract pollinators (mostly birds). Like other Gondwana legends, the waratah is well prepared for fire. It can regenerate, just like eucalypt trees, from a lignotuber growth at its base.

LC

WARATAH (*Telopea speciosissima*)

WARATAHS ARE PROTECTED BY LAW FOR THEIR CULTURAL SIGNIFICANCE TO FIRST NATIONS PEOPLE AND BECAUSE TOO MANY PEOPLE WANT TO PINCH THEIR BEAUTIFUL BLOOMS!

A LIVING FOSSIL, THE ROUGH TREE FERN IS NOT REALLY A TREE BUT IT IS ONE OF OUR MOST ANCIENT PLANTS

LC

ROUGH TREE FERN (*Alsophila australis*)

NORFOLK ISLAND PINE

(*Araucaria heterophylla*)

Native to Norfolk Island, an outer territory of Australia, this pine is not a true pine. Pines from the Laurasia landmass (the *Pinaceae* family) are 'true' but Gondwana pines belong to a different family called *Araucariaceae*. One of the coolest features of the Norfolk Island pine is its branches. Arranged in spirals, they swirl up the trunk, making a pyramid shape. Their unique leaves are needle-like at the top but lower branches can have longer, more pointed leaves.

THIS PINE CAN REACH 60M, OR THE HEIGHT OF A 20-STOREY BUILDING

VU

GREVILLEA

(*Grevillea* spp.)

Also known as spider flowers, grevilleas come in over 300 species. Grevilleas mostly rely on beauty for attention, but some species do have honey or vanilla aromas. The grevillea's brush-like flower heads are masses of individual flowers, each with a long tube called a calyx or style.

BLOOMS ARE BUILT IN MANY WAYS AND THE THREE MOST COMMON TYPES ARE:

SPIDER

BRUSH

TOOTHBRUSH

TO PREVENT WATER LOSS, THE LEAVES OF THE GRANITE GREVILLEA CURL UP IN EXTREME HEAT OR WHEN TOUCHED (CALLED THIGMONASTY)

GRANITE GREVILLEA (*Grevillea neurophylla*)

EN

HAKEAS AND GREVILLEAS ARE SIMILAR, BUT HAKEAS HAVE HARD, WOODY FRUIT WHILE GREVILLEAS HAVE SOFT FRUIT

SOIL MASTERS

Over time, many Gondwanan plants, like species from the Proteaceae family, have adapted to life in nutrient-poor soil by developing cluster (proteoid) roots. These dense, superfine roots have stacks of surface area that can absorb as much water and food as possible.

HAKEA

(*Hakea* spp.)

Hakeas have a huge range of leaf types including flat, needle-like, grassy, fernlike and serrated. To guard against hungry predators, most leaves are stiff with sharp points. Just like grevilleas, their blossoms can grow as single flowers or can bunch up in groups of 100 (or more) to form a flower head. Floral arrangements can vary from pincushion to spider and brush shapes—and some grow along the stems or at the very end.

THE TALLEST WOLLEMI STANDS 40M HIGH AND IS AROUND 1000 YEARS OLD

WOLLEMI PINE

(*Wollemia nobilis*)

In 1994, a park ranger stumbled upon a living fossil—deep in a sandstone canyon northwest of Sydney. The discovery made world news. An ancient conifer from the Jurassic period, the Wollemi pine was thought to be long extinct, so finding it was like discovering a living dinosaur! There are around 100 adult trees in this secret location but to help ensure its survival, botanists have cultivated baby pines that anyone can buy (including you!). Because it's not a true pine, the Wollemi grows 'false' cones. Male cones sit higher up the tree so their pollen falls onto the female cones down below.

HAKEA SEEDS HAVE LEAFY WINGS THAT TAKE OFF ON THE WIND LIKE TINY HELICOPTERS

RED POKERS (*Hakea bucculenta*)

PINCUSHION HAKEA SEED (*Hakea laurina*)

TREES

Australian forests cover 134 million hectares, making them the seventh-largest forest area in the world. Our forest trees are tough. They cope with extreme conditions but they're up for the challenge, especially our eucalypts and acacias. Not only do our trees protect our soil and water, they also remove carbon dioxide from the atmosphere and store carbon in their trunks, leaves and roots. Victoria's mountain ash forests store more carbon than almost any other ecosystem on Earth—even more than the Amazon rainforest!

FAGUS

(*Nothofagus gunnii*)

Australia has a small handful of native deciduous trees and most are found in warmer regions, like red cedar (*Toona ciliata*). In cooler climates, we have just one true deciduous tree—the fagus, which dates back 80 million years and hasn't changed a bit in 35 million years! In autumn, this prehistoric survivor sets Tasmania's hills ablaze with crinkle-cut leaves that change from yellow to orange to red and rusty brown.

LOCALS CALL THIS YEARLY COLOUR CHANGE 'THE TURNING OF THE FAGUS'

FORESTS ARE CONCENTRATED ACROSS THE MAINLAND'S FAR NORTH AND SOUTH WEST, THEN DOWN THE EAST COAST TO TASMANIA

THE BOAB CAN LIVE OVER 1000 YEARS, WHICH IS WHY IT'S CALLED THE TREE OF LIFE

FOREST TYPES

Out native forests are grouped into eight types: **EUCALYPT**, **ACACIA**, **RAINFOREST**, **MELALEUCA** (like tea trees), **CASUARINA** (native pines), **CALLITRIS** (cypress), **MANGROVES** and then all **OTHER** types of tree. More than 80 per cent of Australia's native forest areas are dominated by eucalypt and acacia forest.

GRASS TREE

(*Xanthorrhoea* spp.)

This living fossil dates back 34 million years and all 30 species are found only in Australia. Not a true tree, many species have a stem (called a caudex) covered in stubby, dried leaves, which form a protective layer against fire. Flower spikes are actually triggered by fire and can grow metres tall, with thousands of star-shaped flowers bunched into a flower head. The grass tree is named after its spiky crown that keeps it cool and also channels rainwater into the base of the plant, where it's stored for future use.

LC

THE GRASS TREE GROWS JUST 1CM PER YEAR, SO A TREE AS TALL AS A PRE-SCHOOLER COULD BE 100 YEARS OLD!

USEFUL FLORA

Trees are used for furniture, building, handicrafts, paper production, dyes, resins, medicine and food. Or they can just be enjoyed for their beauty and shade.

IT TAKES AN ASTONISHING 500 YEARS FOR THIS PINE TO REACH ADULTHOOD

HUON PINE

(*Lagarostrobos franklinii*)

Exclusive to Tasmania, the Huon pine is Australia's oldest living tree and the only remaining species in its genus. It's also the second-oldest tree species on Earth, dating back 200 million years. One single tree was dated back 3462 years and the oldest recorded twig fossils are more than 2.6 million years old! Known for its fragrant wood, the Huon is not a true pine but it still sits in the non-flowering group called gymnosperms.

LC

TWIG

POLLEN CONE

LET'S HOPE THE 2024 BAN ON NATIVE LOGGING IN WESTERN AUSTRALIA HELPS SAVE OUR JARRAH GIANTS

JARRAH

(*Eucalyptus marginata*)

This majestic tree stands up to 50m tall and can live 500 years or more. Famous for its hard timber, in the 1880s, slabs of jarrah were shipped to London to make—wait for it—roads. Hard-wearing and resistant to horse pee, these roads became hugely popular, and it wasn't until the end of World War I that logging stopped. Now, most jarrah forests are gone and their precious ecosystems have been ruined.

TIMBER

NT

BOAB

(*Adansonia gregorii*)

This 'upside-down' tree has branches that look like roots and is the only baobab native to Australia. Like a giant water tower, the boab's massive, swollen trunk (up to 5m round) can store an astonishing 100,000 litres of water, which can be tapped for drinking. It's hard to kill a boab. Even after bushfire, it forms new bark, and fallen branches can grow new trunks, just as a root would do. Its large flowers open at night to tempt pollinators like flying foxes and hawk moths.

LC

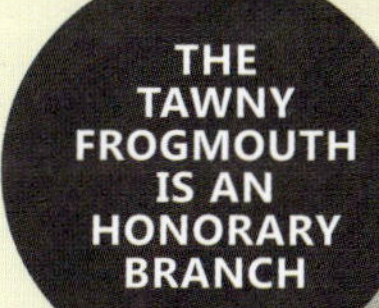

TAWNY FROGMOUTH
(*Podargus strigoides*)

FRIENDLY FAUNA

Animals use trees for shelter, nesting, hunting, hiding and even camouflage. The tawny frogmouth can sit so still, it almost becomes a tree branch. While flying, birds use trees below for navigation, and mammals like the sugar glider use them as travel corridors, leaping from tree to tree.

THIS SHOW PONY KNOWS HOW TO IMPRESS—AND IRRITATE!

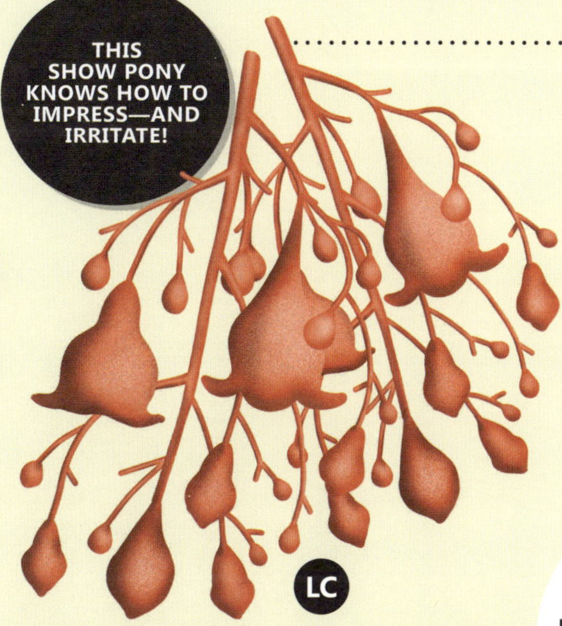

LC

FLAME KURRAJONG

(*Brachychiton acerifolius*)

When the flame kurrajong sheds its leaves, get set for a stunning display of bright red flowers—popping like fireworks all over the canopy. The flower pods are stuffed with seeds covered in irritating hairs, which can cause skin and eye problems. These seeds are also toxic to many animals, including birds, so the tree has to rely on wind pollination.

PAPERY BARK

KUKU YALANJI PEOPLE USED THE SOFT BARK OF THE JIDI (PAPERBARK TREE) TO MAKE FLOOR MATS, ROOFS FOR SHELTER, WATER CONTAINERS AND TO LINE BABY BASKETS. IT WAS ALSO WRAPPED AROUND FISH, EELS AND OTHER FOOD TO FORM A PROTECTIVE LAYER, THEN BAKED OVER FIRE.

TEA TREE

(*Melaleuca alternifolia*)

The world has quickly learned the value of tea tree oil. Although its medicinal properties have long been known by First Nations people, scientists have discovered that the tea tree's antiseptic properties can help with anything from a sore throat to fighting infection. It's also used in many other products like shampoo, skincare and toothpaste.

ALSO CALLED NARROW-LEAVED PAPERBARK, THIS TEA TREE SPECIES IS THE MOST FAMOUS FOR TEA TREE OIL PRODUCTION

LC

GRASSES

One of the largest groups of flowering plants, grasses are also one of the most widespread plant families on Earth. In Australia, they are found all over our land—from savannas and deserts, to woodlands, lakes and beaches.

MIGRATORY LOCUST
(*Locusta migratoria*)

GRASSY SUPER POWERS

We have more than 1000 native grasses, and over time they have developed jaw-dropping survival techniques. Some species can 'remember' past events like fires or locust attack, and can adjust their growing patterns to suit. They can also release organic compounds in times of stress. Neighbouring grasses can 'smell' these compounds and prepare themselves for trouble!

FIRE-ADAPTED

They may appear pretty flammable, but many grasses have evolved to survive fire. Some grow rhizomes (underground stems) that resprout quickly once fire has passed and others have buds that can resprout from their crowns. The seeds of most grasses have hard coats that protect them from heat, while others have specialised biochemical processes that can heal damaged tissue.

SOME GRASSES HAVE FIBROUS ROOTS SO DENSE, THEY MAKE UP 80 PER CENT OF THE PLANT'S WEIGHT!

CULM CROSS SECTION

LC

A BAMBOO STEM IS CALLED A CULM, AND MOST STEMS ARE HOLLOW

GRASSLANDS ARE FOUND ALL OVER AUSTRALIA, WITH FEWER IN THE TROPICS AND THE DRY KATI THANDA–LAKE EYRE BASIN

SOLID GROUND

Grasses have massive, meandering root systems that stabilise the ground, prevent soil erosion and filter water. Almost all species have fibrous roots, and some grow tuber-like rhizomes that help grass regenerate after fire (or too many wombat snack-attacks!). Some species have deep roots that tap into underwater creeks and others can 'sleep' during drought, sometimes waiting many years for the next rain.

BAMBOO

(*Mullerochloa moreheadiana*)

Bamboo is actually a grass and is one of the fastest-growing plants on the planet. Some species can grow a metre a day! Australia's bamboo species are found in tropical regions and include climbing bamboo, which can grow up to 12m tall and up to 60m wide. Some bamboo plants take a long time to flower—up to 120 years!

TUSSOCKS ARE SMALLER CLUMPS OF GRASS. WHEN THEY JOIN TOGETHER, THEY FORM LARGER HUMMOCKS

GRASSLAND TYPES

Our grasses can be grouped into several main types. Here are some examples in each group:

i. **TUSSOCK** Spinifex (*Triodia* spp.)
ii. **HUMMOCK** Porcupine grass (*Triodia scariosa*)
iii. **PASTURE** Kangaroo grass (*Themeda triandra*)
iv. **HIGH RAINFALL** Common reed (*Phragmites australis*)
v. **MITCHELL** Mitchell grass (*Astrebla lappacea*)
vi. **INLAND PLAIN** Windmill grass (*Chloris* spp.)
vii. **WETLANDS** River tussock grass (*Poa labillardierei*)
viii. **COASTAL** Beach spinifex (*Spinifex longifolius*)

i. ii. iii. iv. v. vi. vii. viii.

ALL LC

SPEAR GRASS

(*Austrostipa* spp.)

These grasses are known for bristly seed heads attached to long stems. As the grass sways, seeds catch on the wind, and their clever spear shape allows them to bury easily into the soil (or into your dog's fur or your own bare feet—ouch!).

SPEAR GRASS HAS TOUGH LEAVES THAT PUT OFF HUNGRY HERBIVORES

LC

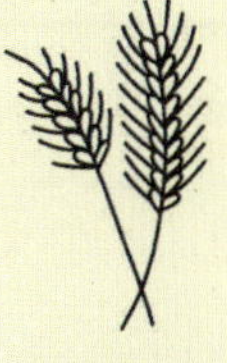

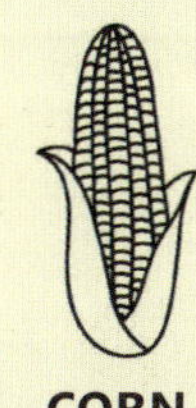

USEFUL FLORA

Grasses are the world's most important source of food—have you heard of wheat, corn and rice? Grasses are also used for paper, textiles, crafts, medicine and roofing.

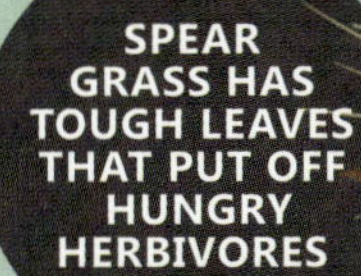

BREATHING UNDERWATER

THE HARD STALKS OF KITJ (IRON GRASS) ARE HOLLOW, SO THE NOONGAR–WUDJARI WOULD FIRST CLEAN AND THEN USE THEM TO BREATHE UNDERWATER, JUST LIKE A SNORKEL. CATCHING DUCKS WAS MADE EASY—THEY WOULD JUST SWIM UNDER THE WATER AND GRAB THE DUCKS BY THEIR FEET!

KANGAROO GRASS

(*Themeda triandra*)

Known for its distinctive seed heads that look like feathery kangaroo tails, this grass thrives in fire-prone environments, with tussocks that can withstand heat, and seeds that can easily germinate when fire has passed.

ROO GRASS THRIVES IN DROUGHT AND ARID REGIONS

LC

FRIENDLY FAUNA

Our native animals use grass for food, protection and nesting material. The male satin bowerbird builds elaborate bowers to attract a mate, using various materials, including grass—along with as many blue objects as he can find!

SPINIFEX PIGEON
(*Geophaps plumifera*)

THIS HARDY GRASS COVERS MORE THAN A QUARTER OF AUSTRALIA, ESPECIALLY THE OUTBACK

SPINIFEX

(*Triodia* spp./*Spinifex* spp.)

We have two types of spinifex—hard and soft—with many species in each group. Porcupine grass (*Triodia scariosa*) has hard, painfully spiky leaves. Few creatures can enter this prickly fortress, but ants, termites and the spinifex pigeon seem to do okay. The common wallaroo is one of the few native animals that actually eat this grass. Its stomach is crammed with microorganisms that can break down such tough, spiny leaves.

LC

BEACH SPINIFEX

(*Spinifex sericeus*)

Beach spinifex comes from the genus *Spinifex* spp., and it's not as scary as its *Triodia* cousin. Its softer, fluffy tussocks dot sand dunes all over Australia, stabilising loose sand and ensuring a healthy ecosystem.

LC

DESERT FLORA

Australia is arid. Our Great Australian Desert (all 10 deserts combined) is an extreme place, copping temperatures up to 50°C in the day, yet dipping below freezing in winter. In 1997, it actually snowed at Uluru! Despite these challenging conditions, flora abounds, with trees, shrubs, succulents, herbs and grasses like spinifex dotting the landscape.

MULGA

(*Acacia aneura*)

Australia's most common tree, the mulga is a shrub or small tree with tiny wattle flowers and needle-like leaves (phyllodes). During drought, they drop their leaves on the ground, which make a protective layer against water loss. Their roots are some of the most extensive of all native trees, and are home to a favourite Anangu bush food—Maku (witchetty grubs).

LC

MULGA TREES COVER ALMOST A QUARTER OF DESERT LAND AND SPINIFEX COVERS ANOTHER QUARTER

DESERT SOIL IS SALTY AND LOW IN NUTRIENTS

STURT'S DESERT ROSE

(*Gossypium sturtianum*)

This sweet little hardcore desert-lover has life in our hottest regions totally under control. Sturt's desert rose copes well with drought thanks to long roots and water stored in its stems and roots. Its large, mauve flowers are also stayers—dotting the barren landscape from winter through summer. Also called the cotton rosebush, this beauty is not actually a rose species—it's a relative of cotton!

LC

STURT'S DESERT ROSE IS THE FLORAL EMBLEM OF THE NORTHERN TERRITORY

HARD SPINIFEX COVERS VAST REGIONS OF OUR DESERT LANDSCAPE

MULGA TREES HAVE DEEP ROOT SYSTEMS THAT START AS A TAP ROOT MEASURING 3M OR MORE—WHEN THE TREE ITSELF IS ONLY A BABY (JUST 20CM TALL!)

THESE ICONIC TREES ARE SO HARDY, THEY CAN LIVE FOR HUNDREDS OF YEARS

COOLIBAH
(*E. coolabah*)

COOLIBAH

(*Eucalyptus coolabah*)

If you see a coolibah tree, there may be water underground, because this tree likes to be close to water and can even cope with flooding. Its rough bark provides heat protection and the epicormic buds beneath the bark can quickly sprout after fire, making it a real desert warrior. You may know Banjo Paterson's song *Waltzing Matilda*, where a jolly swagman camps by a billabong, under the shade of a coolibah tree.

NT

DESERT QUANDONG

(*Santalum acuminatum*)

Totally unrelated to the blue quandong, the scarlet fruit of this desert tree is also called the desert peach and it's packed with vitamins, especially vitamin C. Its seeds look like tiny brains! The Wiradjuri people crack them open and eat the kernels inside. They also stew quandong fruit to make jams and cakes. When dried, the fruit tastes like apricots.

SEED

VU

HEAT STRATEGIES

To conserve water, some plants don't have leaves—they use their stems for photosynthesis (these stems are called phylloclades). Others have very small or water-storing leaves, and plants like the emu bush can curl their leaves to prevent water loss. Longer roots are a clever way to access underground water. Other plants, like mulga acacia (*Acacia aneura*), have tiny leaf hairs that reflect the heat of sunlight. Some, like the boab tree (*Adansonia gregorii*), open their flowers at night, avoiding the scorching heat of the day. During super extreme conditions, some plants go dormant, recovering at the next rain.

BESIDES RAINFALL, THE MAIN SOURCES OF DESERT WATER ARE NATIVE WELLS. CALLED SOAKAGES, THEY CAN BE DUG INTO FOR PRECIOUS H_2O

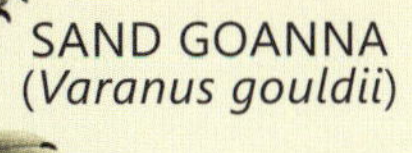

SAND GOANNA (*Varanus gouldii*)

KATI THANDA–LAKE EYRE IS USUALLY DRY, FILLING ONLY TWICE EACH CENTURY!

DYING FOR A DRINK

Our combined deserts receive less than 250mm of rainfall each year. That's just one bathtub of water for an area measuring 2,700,000km^2. Yep. Even thunderstorms are mostly just lightning cracks and thunder rumbles, without a single drop of rain, and when the rains do come, an entire year's worth could fall in one month or even one day! Our driest region of all is the Kati Thanda–Lake Eyre basin. If it does rain, the land is quickly transformed into a kaleidoscope of blooms and wetland foliage.

FRIENDLY FAUNA

In a place where living is tough, native animals have found clever ways to eat and use our flora, even adapting specialised digestion to cope with tough grasses—like the antilopine wallaroo (*Macropus antilopinus*). The sand goanna (*Varanus gouldii*) uses mulga trees like a living pantry, climbing up in search of birds' eggs.

STICKY SPINIFEX

WIRADJURI PEOPLE USE THE RESIN OF DYURIGALGAL MUGARR (SPINIFEX) AS A GLUE FOR TOOLS AND WEAPONS LIKE THE WOOMERA (SPEAR THROWER) AND SPEAR TIPS. THEY HEAT THE RESIN TO MAKE A TAR-LIKE GLUE. WHEN LATER REHEATED OR CHEWED, IT BECOMES LIKE PLASTICINE.

HONEY GREVILLEA

(*Grevillea eriostachya*)

In winter and spring, this grevillea sprouts spikes of bright yellow and green flowers—a favourite of local birds. The flowers are loaded with thick, honey-like nectar which you can lick from the blooms!

LC

LONG-LEAVED EMU BUSH

(*Eremophila longifolia*)

Our emu bush species get their names from emus, who make short work of their fruit! These plants are expert desert dwellers, with amazing defences against drought. The long-leaved emu bush grows in many difficult habitats, including rocky hills, sand plains and sand dunes. Researchers have discovered infection-busting properties in its leaves that are as effective as modern antibiotics.

LC

WATER FLORA

Australia may be dry—but our waterways thrive with native flora. From tiny creeks to our mighty Murray River, wetlands include mangroves, lakes, coral reefs and surrounding seas. Water plants protect our shores, absorb pollution and carbon, improve water quality, produce stacks of oxygen and provide happy habitats for animals.

WATER FLORA TYPES

Whether salt, freshwater or a mixture of both, water flora comes in three main types:

- **EMERGENT** have stems, leaves and flowers above the water's surface.
- **SUBMERGENT** are completely covered by water, with roots attached to mud, sand or rocks.
- **FLOATING** move freely on or beneath the water's surface. They have floating, anchored or no true roots at all.

WETLAND WONDER

THE CUMBUNGI (NATIVE BULRUSH) THRIVES IN FLOODS. THE ROOTS CAN BE PEELED OR DRIED FOR DAMPER, THE LONG LEAVES CAN BE WOVEN INTO MATS, BASKETS AND ROPE, AND THE STEMS CAN BE USED TO MAKE LIGHT SPEARS. THE WIRADJURI PEOPLE USED THESE SPEARS TO HUNT FOR WETLAND BIRDS AND ANIMALS.

PROTISTS VS CHROMISTS

Algae is not technically a plant. It belongs to groups (called Protista and Chromista) that sometimes look like plants but don't have true roots, stems or leaves. Some protists and chromists, including seaweeds, produce food through photosynthesis, just like plants do!

FREE-FLOATERS

Fully aquatic plants have thin, flexible stems. Their roots attach to the muddy bottom or dangle freely, sucking nutrients straight from the water. Other species form dense floating mats (called colonies) that bustle with insects, fish and amphibians, and some have air-filled tissue or sacs to help them float.

LC

NARDOO

(Marsilea drummondii)

An aquatic fern, nardoo's clover-like leaves float gently on the water's surface. Spores are made in protective capsules, and when water dries up, they fall into the cracks of drying mud where they can wait as long as 30 years for the next rain. Even in deserts, if rare rains or floods appear, nardoo quickly resprouts.

THIS LOTUS HAS HYDROPHOBIC LEAVES, SO WATER SIMPLY ROLLS OFF, TAKING DIRT WITH IT—SORT OF LIKE AN AUTOMATIC PLANT WASH!

SACRED LOTUS

(Nelumbo nucifera)

This sweet-smelling lotus bears one of our largest wildflowers. When ripe, its flat seed pod dries up and drops into the water where it floats around, releasing fruit. Each one sinks into the rich mud below, later sprouting into baby plants. Amazingly, the sacred lotus can adjust its own temperature (thermoregulate).

GIANT KELP

(Macrocystis pyrifera)

The largest and fastest-growing marine 'plant' is not really a plant, it's a brown algae (Chromista), yet giant kelp can grow as big as trees! In fact, it forms huge underwater forests with canopies reaching the ocean's surface. Like all seaweeds, its leaves (blades), stems (stipes) and roots (holdfasts) are not true leaves, stems and roots. Its holdfast oozes a sticky substance that helps it cling to rocks below, and because it has no roots, the kelp absorbs food through its blades. Giant kelp has air-filled bladders that help its fronds float upwards, reaching for the sunlight it needs for photosynthesis.

AIR BLADDER

EN

GIANT SWORD SEDGE (*Gahnia grandis*)

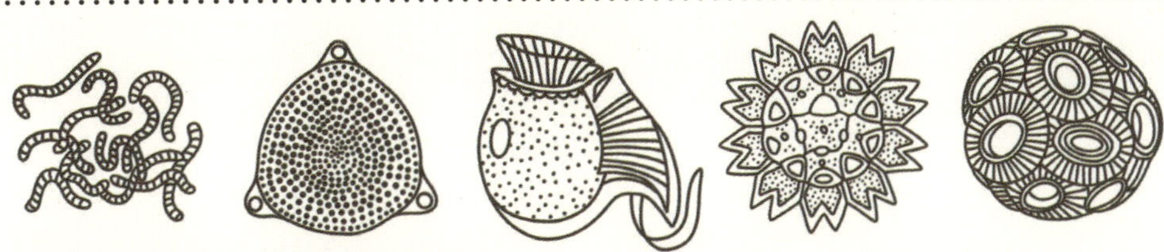

PHYTOPLANKTON

There are one quintillion (1,000,000,000,000,000,000) phytoplankton in the world's oceans, and although they represent just one per cent of our plants, they produce more than half the world's oxygen. Most phytoplankton are microscopic, but when they band together, they form gigantic 'blooms' that can be seen from space!

LAND THAT MINGLES WITH WATERWAYS IS CALLED RIPARIAN

GRASSES

Water-loving grasses anchor on the banks of waterbodies, filtering water, stabilising soil and forming animal homes with water views. The giant sword sedge may be a reed, but it's still part of the grass family. It can grow over 2m high, with clumps of thin, sword-like leaves, hollow stems and inflorescent flowers.

MANGROVES

Mangroves straddle land and sea, in conditions that would kill most plants. They have special glands on their leaves that filter salt, and grow pneumatophore roots to survive in airless, muddy water. These roots act like woody snorkels, sucking in oxygen! We have 41 species of mangrove—from 19 completely different plant families. How? When mangroves first appeared 100 million years ago, they evolved in different parts of the world at the same time (called convergent evolution). More than half the world's mangrove species now live in Australia, and the white mangrove is the most common.

MANGROVE SEEDS GERMINATE ON THE TREE THEN DROP INTO THE WATER AS SEEDLINGS, FLOATING AWAY TO GROW ELSEWHERE

WHITE MANGROVE (*Avicennia marina*)

LC

PNEUMATOPHORE ROOTS

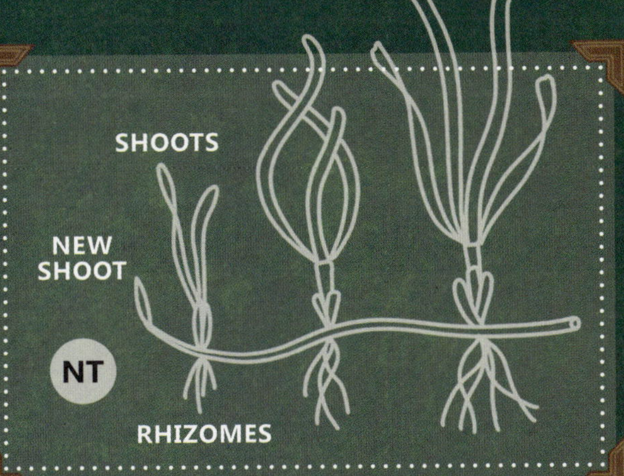

RIBBON WEED

(*Posidonia australis*)

This astonishing weed can reproduce from both its flowers and its rhizomes, and can form large, long-lived meadows that can be hundreds of years old. But one large patch in Shark Bay, Western Australia, covers a massive 200km^2 of shallow ocean floor and is considered the world's largest living plant! It's a single plant because it has self-cloned for at least 4500 years.

RIBBON WEED PLAYS A BIG ROLE IN SHAPING AND STRENGTHENING COASTAL ECOSYSTEMS

SCI-FI FLORA

Don't head to the cinema for a science-fiction fix—just take a walk in nature! These astonishing plants might seem like they're from Mars, but they live in our own backyard—all the way from the Top End down to Tasmania.

MISTLETOE

(Nuytsia floribunda)

Forget kissing under the mistletoe in Europe—Australia is the real home of mistletoe, with the most species on Earth. Our Christmas tree is the world's largest parasitic plant and is one of the few mistletoes that grow as a tree, not a shrub. This freeloader doesn't get its nutrients from the barren soil ... it sends roots up to 150m in search of a host, then grows a ring (haustoria) around a victim's root. The haustoria contains—wait for it—sharp wooden 'blades'! These sever the host root so the tree can attach its own root and steal food and water.

LC

THIS MISTLETOE TREE CAN EVEN CUT POWER AND TELEPHONE LINES!

WIRADJURI CHILDREN LOVE THE MISTLETOE'S SWEET, GRAPE-LIKE FRUIT, CALLED 'SNOTTY GOBBLES'!

STRANGLER FIG

(Ficus virens)

One of the biggest moochers in the plant kingdom, strangler figs take it all—the food, the top floor apartment and the basement, too. When birds eat then poop this fig's seeds into trees below, the seedlings flourish ... with deadly plans. Like all stranglers, the white fig sends curling roots down and around the host tree's stem, anchoring into the ground to steal nutrients. Soon, the victim gasps its last breath ... and dies.

LC

INSIDE-OUT FLOWERS

The flowers and pollen of figs are hidden inside their fruit! A female wasp crawls inside the fig, lays her eggs and dies. When the babies mature, they chew their way out and carry pollen to the next fig.

DON'T WORRY, THE FIGS WE EAT ARE FROM WASP-FREE SPECIES ... OR ARE THEY?

RED AND GREEN KANGAROO PAW

(Anigozanthos manglesii)

Like fuzzy zombie paws, this plant's velvety flowers arch up from the earth, forming the perfect perch for long-beaked birds. Stalks can grow over a metre tall and the slender, grass-like leaves can survive long periods without rain. This roo paw is Western Australia's state flower, and like many Aussie plants, it can survive fire thanks to underground stems (rhizomes).

THYNNID WASP (*Thynnid* spp.)

THIS DANCE BETWEEN ORCHID AND WASP IS A GREAT EXAMPLE OF CO-EVOLUTION

HAMMER ORCHID

(Drakaea elastica)

The only way a hammer orchid can pollinate is with the help of thynnid wasps. So, of course, the head of this orchid just happens to look and smell like a female thynnid wasp! It has a hinged section that bobs up and down like a hammer, and when a male wasp tries to mate with this fake female, the hammer-like petal drops down and traps the male. As he struggles to escape, he's dredged in pollen before zooming off to fertilise another plant.

CRANBROOK BELL

(Darwinia meeboldii)

With its furry-looking, spindly branches and toothy blossoms, this bell may look like a people-eater, but fear not! What looks like tentacles are just very, very leafy stems—with no teeth at all. Inside these pink and white bells are eight small and very harmless flowers, made of bracts, not knives.

STURT'S DESERT PEA

(Swainsona formosa)

The trailing stems of this extra-terrestrial pea swirl and creep over the barren Outback. Each flower's haunted black eye (called a 'boss') acts like a barrier to prevent small insects from stealing pollen. This is because the desert pea prefers pollinators with a long proboscis or beak that can reach into its flowers. The petals of this desert species are shaped a bit like a yacht—with a standard petal, a keel and two wings.

FIREWOOD BANKSIA

(Banksia menziesii)

Despite its pretty blooms, this nest of saw-blade leaves might be a little alarming to stumble upon on a moonless night. These leaves can reach almost half a metre in length and are covered in a waxy layer and fine, white hairs that reflect the sun's rays. This hard-core stunner sacrifices itself for its seeds, which need fire to germinate. Don't get too close—you may be dragged in and devoured!

FRINGED HELMET ORCHID

(Corybas fimbriatus)

Is it a plant or a blood-sucking Martian tick? Whatever it is, don't worry—it's teensy! A single leaf supports this odd little orchid with its petal fringes that look a bit like insect legs. Bees are lured by the orchid's earthy aroma. They transfer pollen as they pop in and out of the flower.

THE BURRAWANG IS A DESCENDANT OF EARTH'S VERY FIRST FLOWERING PLANTS (CYCAD FERNS)

BURRAWANG

(Macrozamia communis)

The burrawang dates back 200 million years. It may look like a fern from a dinosaur movie, but it's not—it's related to conifers! Plants are either male or female. The male has long, narrow cones packed with pollen and the female has a larger cone that breaks open to spill enormous seeds. The burrawang grows just a few new leaves each year and can live to count hundreds of birthday candles.

DEADLY FLORA

Plants may seem rather harmless, but many produce a witch's cauldron of harsh and even deadly chemicals to help protect themselves against attack. Some animals have developed immunity, while many others, including us, have not. Thankfully, our toxic flora isn't that appealing to us (so happy mangoes aren't toxic!). Poisoning is rare and usually by accident, but this is why we can't eat (or sometimes even touch!) plants we're unfamiliar with. Here are some plants that might give you nightmares. Read on if you dare ...

BAT'S WING CORAL TREE

(*Erythrina vespertilio*)

Part of the pea family, this tropical tree is named after its pretty coral flowers and leaves that flutter like flying bats. Don't be fooled by pretty, though. Deadly toxins are found in the leaves and bark of the coral tree, and most especially the seeds. On top of that, the tree's trunk and branches are covered in sharp, rose-like thorns. Small branches often drop to the ground and can wound barefoot wanderers!

LC

THIS IS ONE DEFENSIVE PLANT!

WHITE CEDAR

(*Melia azedarach var. australasica*)

This tree has lovely timber and pretty clusters of fragrant flowers. It's the fruit that rears its ugly head, with a complex blend of poisons including neurotoxins that can cause seizures and even coma. Birds have somehow developed immunity because the tree relies on them to eat their fruit and disperse seed in their droppings. Now, that's some kind of co-evolutionary cleverness!

WARNING!

UNDER THE MICROSCOPE

STINGING NETTLE

(*Urtica incisa*)

While not deadly, the stinging nettle is still painful. Its tiny hairs release histamines, which cause pain, itching and redness—yet tender young nettles can actually be eaten! Cooking or drying out the leaves destroys the hairs and they can be made into delicious tea and soup, or even blanched and added to salads or pizza!

CHECK WITH AN ADULT BEFORE EATING ANY UNKNOWN PLANT

BUNYA PINE

(*Araucaria bidwillii*)

The bunya pine may look beautiful and even harmless, but its cones are bigger than footballs and can weigh a massive 10kg. These cones drop without warning and can fall as far as 50m. You certainly don't want one landing on your head! This pine is sacred to the Gubbi Gubbi people. It can't be harmed, so only one person is now authorised to cut and mill the timber.

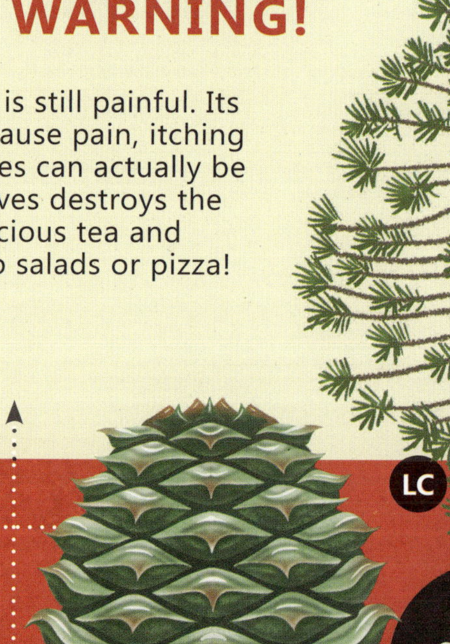

THE SLOW-GROWING BUNYA CAN REACH 500 YEARS!

ROSARY PEA

(*Abrus precatorius*)

The seeds of this supposedly 'sweet' pea may look like ladybirds—but they're actually capable of murder. Immature seeds, or even those with a tiny scratch, can release a deadly poison, and just a tiny part of each seed is enough to kill a human. In fact, breathing in the poison is even more dangerous, but the rosary pea doesn't care! It's out to conquer the world, spreading all over the planet's tropical regions and down into the southern hemisphere—including Queensland where it has become naturalised.

THE TOP END STONEFISH IS ONE OF THE ONLY KNOWN ANIMALS THAT CAN SAFELY EAT ROSARY PEA SEEDS

LC

ROSARY PEA SEEDS ARE OFTEN USED TO MAKE JEWELLERY, BUT EVEN POKING HOLES THROUGH THESE SEEDS IS DANGEROUS!

EATING EVEN A TINY PIECE CAN BE DEADLY, SO THE BOTTOM LINE IS: NEVER EAT A WILD MUSHROOM OF ANY KIND ... EVER!

DEATH CAP MUSHROOM

(*Amanita phalloides*)

Mushrooms are not plants—they are types of fungi in a plant-like form. In fact, they are the fruit-like part of fungi's main body, which is made up of a network of threads called mycelia. These mushroomy 'fruits' make reproductive spores in the gills underneath their caps, so it's easy to mistake them for a type of plant. They're still worth a mention because some people treat them like plants, and it's good to know if death caps are growing in your garden. These mushies are highly toxic and are responsible for many poisonings.

LC

EUCALYPT THUGS

Eucalyptus trees can sometimes shed a branch or two, with zero notice. Known as 'sudden branch drop', this only really happens during drought, disease or severe stress. The thing to remember is that many types of tree occasionally drop branches, and the reason our eucalypts get a bad rap is because they make up most of the trees in our country!

FORGET ABOUT DROP BEARS—IT'S BRANCHES YOU NEED TO WATCH OUT FOR

WATER TRAP

NOONGAR–WUDJARI PEOPLE USE THE RATHER HARMLESS-LOOKING KANDYAP YOOLBA (BLIND GRASS) TO POISON WATERHOLES. AFTER DRINKING THE WATER, ANIMALS LIKE KANGAROOS FALL ASLEEP AND QUICKLY BECOME LUNCH!

GYMPIE GYMPIE

(*Dendrocnide moroides*)

Known as the most painful plant on Earth, just a light touch of the gympie gympie can feel like acid, fire and electrocution—all at the same time. How? The plant's fine little hairs (called trichomes) are like nature's hypodermic needles. When they enter the skin, they inject their fiery venom ... and the pain can last for months. But don't worry—just avoid the rainforests between Cape York Peninsula and northern New South Wales, and you'll be fine! And if you can't avoid these areas, be sure to wear long pants when walking in the bush.

UNDER THE MICROSCOPE

EN

CURIOUSER AND CURIOUSER

Australian flora is definitely unique, but some species take things to a whole new level, with unusual or bizarre looks, clever tricks and astonishing adaptations—like becoming their very own water tank. Our country may not be known for succulents, but the fleshy species we do have are pretty cool. Our plants can even eat meat! Yep—Australia is home to more carnivorous plants than anywhere else in the world.

UNDER THE MAGNIFYING GLASS

Some plants are very hard to see. Phytoplankton may be the largest plant group on Earth but they're also the smallest, just a few micrometres in size. Other itty-bitty plants include bryophytes (liverworts, hornworts, mosses) and teensy tiny ferns. The Pacific mosquito fern (*Azolla filiculoides*) has fronds just a few millimetres wide (3000 micrometres).

ONE MICROMETRE IS ONE MILLIONTH OF A METRE. HOW SMALL IS THAT? WELL, THE HEAD OF A PIN MEASURES A WHOPPING 2000 MICROMETRES ACROSS

SUCCULENTS

Succulents can store water in their leaves, stems and roots, making desert life a whole lot easier. Most species have a special form of photosynthesis called CAM (crassulacean acid metabolism). At night, when it's cooler, they use CAM to draw in carbon and store it as acid in their cells, just like a battery. When the sun rises again, these acids break down into the carbon dioxide needed for photosynthesis. Clever!

LARGE-ARTICLED SAMPHIRE

(*Tecticornia bulbosa*)

This native has strange, barrel-shaped segments (called articles) that can change from green to pale blue, pink and red. Its flowers are hermaphroditic, meaning it needs no boyfriend or girlfriend—it just self-pollinates (called autogamy). Found along salty coastlines, this samphire thrives in places most plants fear to tread. It's nicknamed 'pickleweed' for its tangy flavour, and its stems can be pickled, just like cucumbers!

SALT-LOVING PLANTS ARE CALLED HALOPHYTIC

VU

PLANTS ALIVE!

Plants collect information. They can sense light and some can even follow the movement of the sun across the sky (known as heliotropism). They can make use of magnetism and electricity, and can sense temperature, vibrations, nutrients, moisture—even gravity. Plants also 'talk' to each other. They release chemicals to warn nearby pals that hungry beetles are on the way!

PINK PIGFACE

(*Carpobrotus glaucescens*)

One of our few true succulents, this beach-loving creeper holds sand dunes together and is a surprising food source. Its leaves, fruit and ultra-pink flowers have a salty-sweet taste. The green pigface (*Gunniopsis septifraga*) has modified leaves that look like large lollies. It changes colour during times of stress.

THIS JELLY BEAN GROWS LIKE A ROSETTE THEN MEANDERS UP TO 80CM OVER THE GROUND

JELLY BEAN PLANT

(*Calandrinia creethae*)

This cool plant comes in a variety of candy colours, with leaves like plump jelly beans. It may seem delicate, but this jelly bean thrives in the desert by storing water in its stems and closing its blossoms at night. Many wildlife species love this plant, including emu chicks, who totally rely on it for their first six weeks of life.

LC

CARNIVOROUS PLANTS

Our carnivorous plants live almost everywhere—from forests to billabongs and deserts. Alison Baird Reserve south of Perth covers just 35 hectares, yet it has more carnivorous plants than Europe! These minuscule munchers catch flying insects and sometimes snails and caterpillars. They occasionally (by accident!) catch small frogs, birds and mammals, which can't be digested.

IF YOU'RE EVER TRAPPED BY A CARNIVOROUS PLANT, DON'T PANIC! JUST STAY STILL AND THE PLANT WILL SOON OPEN ITS JAWS TO RELEASE YOU

WATERWHEEL PLANT

(Aldrovanda vesiculosa)

This underwater version of the Venus fly trap doesn't need roots because its food arrives alive and kicking. When its modified leaves are triggered by prey, they snap shut (in 20 milliseconds) then slowly digest lunch before popping open again for the next meal. Its floating leaves resemble the blades of a waterwheel.

UNDER THE MICROSCOPE

CR

ALBANY PITCHER PLANT

(Cephalotus follicularis)

This little dinosaur has been around for 55 million years and is our smallest pitcher plant, with traps just 4cm high. It has a completely different ancestry to other pitchers and is more closely related to cabbage! Like other pitcher plants, its traps are made from modified leaves that form a sort of bucket. Insects slip into the liquid below, which is packed with digestive enzymes that break down prey.

VU

JUST 20 SMALL GROUPS OF THE ALBANY PITCHER PLANT REMAIN, ALL NEAR ALBANY IN WESTERN AUSTRALIA

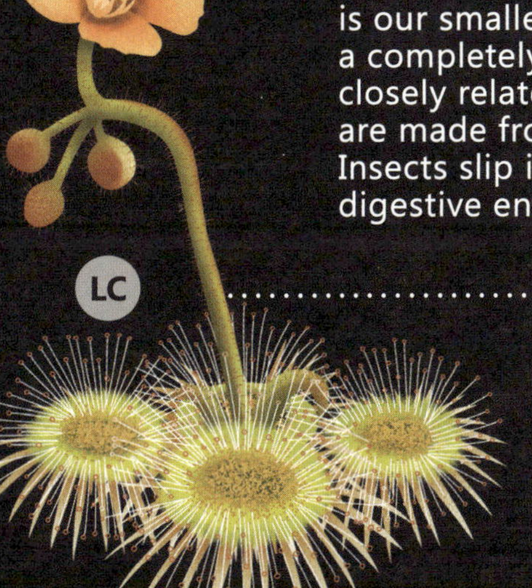

LC

PIMPERNEL SUNDEW

(Drosera glanduligera)

Sundews are one of the largest groups of carnivorous plants. This unique species actually has two types of trap—flypaper and snaptrap. Its leaves are covered in sticky flytrap tentacles, and when an insect lands, the snap-tentacles around the edge of each leaf push it onto the flytrap tentacles in the centre (where digestion can begin). Unlike some other snaptrap plants, once a tentacle snaps down, it can't come back up again.

ENTRAPMENT

Most carnivorous plants are found in nutrient-poor soils and so have come up with inventive ways to find lunch. Although they have no teeth (yet!), they have evolved several types of trap:

- **FLYPAPER** Victims are lured by sticky droplets, and when they land, they're instantly stuck.
- **PITFALL** A bucket-like container made from a modified leaf full of digestive fluid. Prey slips in and becomes soup!
- **BLADDER** Bladderworts (*Utricularia*) grow tiny bladders on their roots. When micro prey get close, the bladder's flap flips open and prey is sucked inside at a speed of 60 G-forces, making them the world's fastest plant!
- **SNAP** Leaves and tentacles are touch-sensitive, closing on prey in the blink of an eye. This movement is thanks to an electrochemical process that rapidly alters leaf cells.

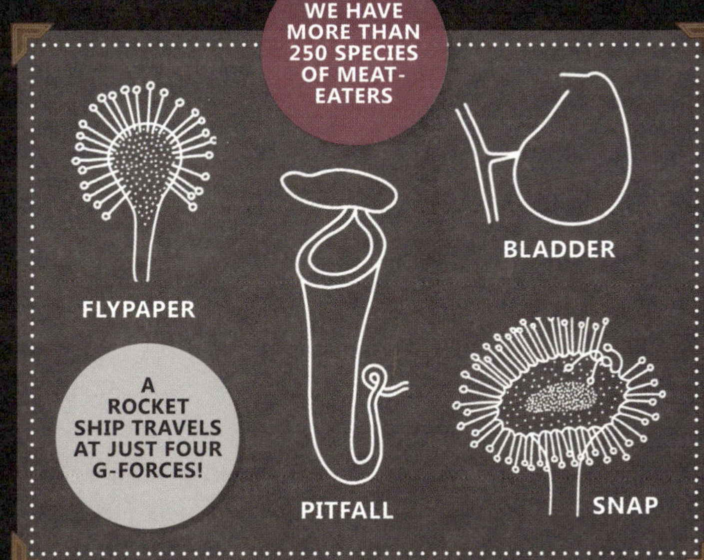

OUR WILD FLOWERS

Australia has the world's greatest diversity of wildflower, with over 60 per cent found nowhere else on Earth. Over half are unique to Western Australia, which is famous for its stunning displays. From winter through early spring, wild blossoms turn sweeping savannas into a magic carpet of colour. They are found in other places, too, from deserts to rainforests to Mount Kosciuszko, where white snow daisies and bright yellow billy buttons flourish in summer.

LC

CALLISTEMON

(*Callistemon* spp.)

The iconic bottlebrush has more than 50 species, from dwarf shrubs to 10m trees, like the weeping bottlebrush. Their flower heads are really a series of tiny blooms that pop from buds along the stem. Each full flower head has lashings of nectar that can be licked from the blooms—like nature's lollipop!

WEEPING BOTTLEBRUSH
(*Callistemon viminalis*)

CALLISTEMON IS LATIN FOR 'BEAUTIFUL STAMENS'

BILLY BUTTONS

(*Pycnosorus globosus*)

From the daisy family, this adorable yellow button is a colour-pop in clumps of woolly leaves. Its flowers are a collection of teeny blossoms all bunched together to form a ball. Because billy buttons grow from an underground rhizome, they can resprout quickly after fire.

LC

UNDER THE MICROSCOPE

LC

EVERLASTING DAISY

(*Xerochrysum bracteatum*)

Also called strawflower or paper daisy, this crisp bloom comes in a kaleidoscope of colour. Its papery petals are actually bracts (modified leaves), but are they everlasting? Smaller blooms can last many months and larger ones up to six years! This darling daisy closes at night and also if it rains.

THIS DAISY CONTINUES TO OPEN AND CLOSE, EVEN WHEN PICKED

LILLY PILLY

(*Syzygium* spp.)

Lilly pilly species can vary from small shrubs to large trees. They have fluffy flowers and glossy green leaves that can start out pink or red. Many lilly pillys have delicious berries, some with a sweet cranberry taste, while others are sour or even spicy!

LC

FLOWER LOVERS

Wildflowers and native bees have an electric relationship. Flowers are negatively charged and bees are positively charged, so when a bee lands, it feels a soft little zap. This could help the bee remember the flower, so it returns over and over again.

TEDDY BEAR BEE
(*Amegilla bombiformis*)

CUCKOO BEE
(*Thyreus nitidulus*)

BLUE-BANDED BEE
(*Amegilla cingulata*)

GERALDTON WAX

(*Chamelaucium uncinatum*)

Geraldton wax gets its name from its drought-tolerant, waxy leaves. It has unusual, bowl-like petals and leathery, needle-like leaves that have a citrusy scent when crushed. Its flower buds can be pink, purple or white—and they smell like honey.

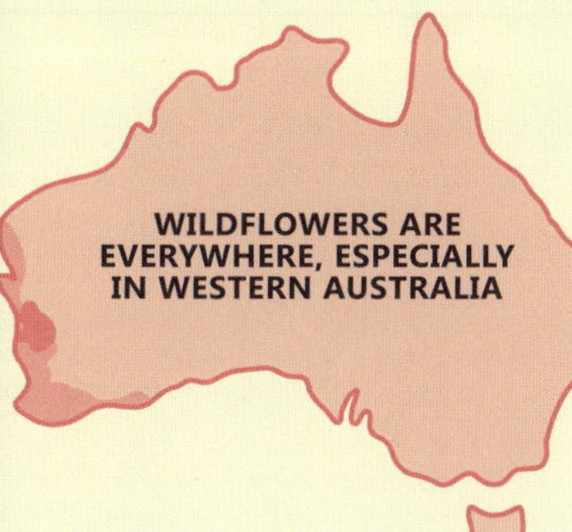

PINK MULLA MULLA

(*Ptilotus exaltatus*)

Mulla mullas produce masses of flower spikes, often over a metre high. Each flower head consists of tiny blossoms surrounded by fluffy white hairs, so no wonder they're nicknamed 'pussy tails'! When ready, these pretty heads sail off on the wind, spreading seeds far and wide.

FLANNEL FLOWERS USE SMOKE-INDUCED GERMINATION

FLANNEL FLOWER

(*Actinotus helianthi*)

This soft, woolly flower may be covered in fine hairs, but its petals aren't what they seem—they're actually bracts surrounding a ball of teensy flowers. Flannel flower seeds can detect smoke! At the very first whiff, seeds on the ground start sprouting, taking advantage of the nutritious soil left after fires.

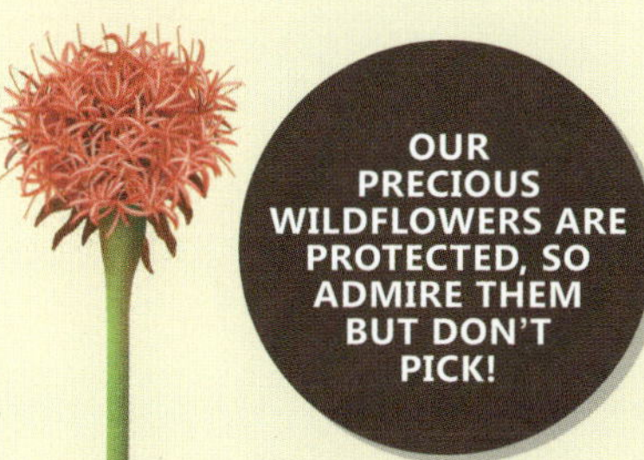

PINCUSHION HAKEA

(*Hakea laurina*)

The glamour puss of the botanical world, this large shrub has leathery leaves and striking, honey-scented pompom flowers. Like many hakea species, these flowers are a mass of tiny, tightly packed tubular blooms, studded with as many as 190 pins (stamens).

GYMEA LILY

(*Doryanthes excelsa*)

The gymea lily has a long-lasting flower spike that can grow as high as 6m, making it one of the tallest in the plant kingdom. At the top of the spike, a cluster of red, nectar-plumped flowers can reach a whopping 30cm in diameter, but this lily is so long lived and slow growing, it can take 10 years for flowers to appear.

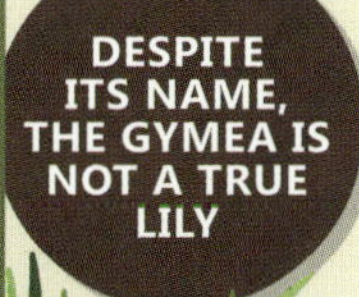

LC

GRASS TRIGGER PLANT

(*Stylidium schoenoides*)

Trigger plants are easily triggered. When bees land on a flower, the plant's style flicks forward, dashing pollen onto the bee's back. Pollen is precious and each plant needs to attract the perfect pollinator, so the trigger of this clever plant has adapted to suit the weight of a bee.

BUSH FOOD

It's easy to fall in love with native ingredients. Bush food (previously called bush tucker) is not only delicious, it's nutritious, sustainable and includes native plants traditionally harvested by First Nations people. Bush food may taste brand new or familiar—from tart finger limes that seem a little grapefruity to nutty wattleseeds with notes of spice, coffee, raisins and chocolate. Yum!

ALL OF THIS BUSH FOOD IS LEAST CONCERN (LC) EXCEPT THE PENCIL YAM, WHICH IS ENDANGERED (EN)

WATTLESEED

(*Acacia* spp.)

An important source of protein, wattleseeds are enjoyed by Wiradjuri people, who roast and grind them into flour to make damper and Johnny cakes. With a savoury, nutty flavour, they are also scrumptious in foods like ice cream and scrambled eggs.

NOT ALL SPECIES OF ACACIA HAVE EDIBLE SEEDS

LEMON MYRTLE

(*Backhousia citriodora*)

With a fresh, zesty lemon flavour, this herb is used fresh or ground into a powder. It's delicious in desserts, sauces, syrups and teas.

LEMON MYRTLE HAS ALMOST 10 TIMES THE AMOUNT OF CITRAL (LEMON SCENT) THAN LEMONS!

PENCIL YAM

(*Dioscorea transversa*)

Also called finger yams, the roots of this rare, climbing plant really do look like long, knobbly fingers. Growing up to a metre below ground, they are delicious roasted.

BAKED PENCIL YAMS TASTE LIKE ROAST POTATO

EN

BUSH TOMATO

(*Solanum centrale*)

This small, tangy tomato has a punchy, sweet yet savoury flavour. High in vitamin C, it's used in chutneys and sauces, or ground into a spice. Don't eat too many, though. Noongar–Wudjari people say it could give you a belly ache.

WHEN THE BUSH TOMATO IS DRIED, IT'S CALLED A RAISIN

KAKADU PLUM

(*Terminalia ferdinandiana*)

This plum is one of the world's richest sources of vitamin C. It has a tangy, sour and sometimes salty flavour, and makes tasty jams, chutneys, sauces, drinks and desserts.

WARNING!

SOME PLANTS ARE TOXIC AND COULD MAKE YOU VERY ILL, SO NEVER EAT ANY PLANT YOU'RE UNFAMILIAR WITH

KAKADU PLUMS HAVE 100 TIMES MORE VITAMIN C THAN ORANGES

MACADAMIA NUTS

(*Macadamia integrifolia*)

Famous worldwide for their rich, buttery flavour, macadamia nuts are used in cooking and baking, to make oil or just as a delicious snack. Their seed coats are so hard, you will definitely need an elephant to help you open them.

SCOTT'S GINGER

(*Hornstedtia scottiana*)

This edible rhizome tastes a bit like regular ginger. The fleshy flower spike can be peeled like a banana to reach the sweet seeds inside. Kuku Yalanji children love these seeds, but to stop them being eaten before they are ripe, elders warn the seeds can cause thunderstorms and lightning!

FINGER LIME

(*Citrus australasica*)

A rainforest citrus fruit, the finger lime bursts with beads (called pearls) packed with citrusy juice. High in vitamin C, they're used to garnish both sweet and savoury dishes.

BUSH COCONUT

(*Corymbia opaca*)

The bush coconut comes from an unusual (and perhaps a little icky!) dance between the desert bloodwood tree and a grublike insect (*Cystococcus*). A female grub chooses a spot on a tree branch and starts scratching. To defend itself, the tree grows a knobby tumour (gall) around the grub, who happily spends the rest of her life inside, gobbling sap and welcoming mates via a tiny air hole. Both the gall and the grub form the 'bush coconut' and the Ngarluma people say its thick white lining tastes like—you guessed it—coconut!

RIVER MINT

(*Mentha australis*)

The leaves of this native have a strong peppermint flavour and can be used fresh or dried. They are used in teas and to add flavour to both sweet and savoury dishes. Try it in sparkling water with a squeeze of lemon.

FLORAL EMBLEMS

Flowers are not just a pretty face—they have deeper meanings and are used in many symbolic ways. Wildflowers are used for food, medicine, perfume, oils, education, research, and cultural and traditional purposes. Or ... for simply admiring.

STATE AND TERRITORY FLORA

Each state and territory abounds with wildflowers, yet each one also has its own floral emblem. These blooms may be used on a flag or coat of arms, on government letters and websites, or even featured in local events and festivals.

- **NEW SOUTH WALES** Waratah
- **VICTORIA** Pink heath
- **QUEENSLAND** Cooktown orchid
- **SOUTH AUSTRALIA** Sturt's desert pea
- **WESTERN AUSTRALIA** Red and green kangaroo paw
- **TASMANIA** Tasmanian blue gum
- **NORTHERN TERRITORY** Sturt's desert rose
- **AUSTRALIAN CAPITAL TERRITORY** Royal bluebell

OUR STATE AND TERRITORY FLORAL EMBLEMS ARE ENDEMIC TO AUSTRALIA—WHICH MEANS FOUND NOWHERE ELSE ON EARTH

FLORAL WAR

In the 1900s, a war was fought for our national floral emblem. Team wattle and team waratah battled it out all over the country, but team wattle won. Why? Because just like Australia's people, the wattle is found all over the country, while the waratah is only found on the east coast.

GOLDEN NATION

Australia's national floral emblem is the golden wattle. It can be found on our coat of arms and there is a species of wattle on each of our banknotes. Our national flower is reflected in our national sporting teams, who often wear green and gold.

BROWN BORONIA
(*Boronia megastigma*)

ON THE NOSE

Timber, bark, leaves, stems and roots have aromas too, with leaves the strongest. The leaves of the curry myrtle and bush mint smell like their name and the underground stem of native ginger has a spicy scent and taste. Australia's boronias are famously fragrant.

***NOTE** October's flower, the protea (left), is not Australian. It's native to South Africa.

WILDFLOWER MEANINGS

Blooms all over the world are given special meanings—like a sort of language. Different countries have their own floral language, but these beloved Aussie wildflowers have their own native language, too.

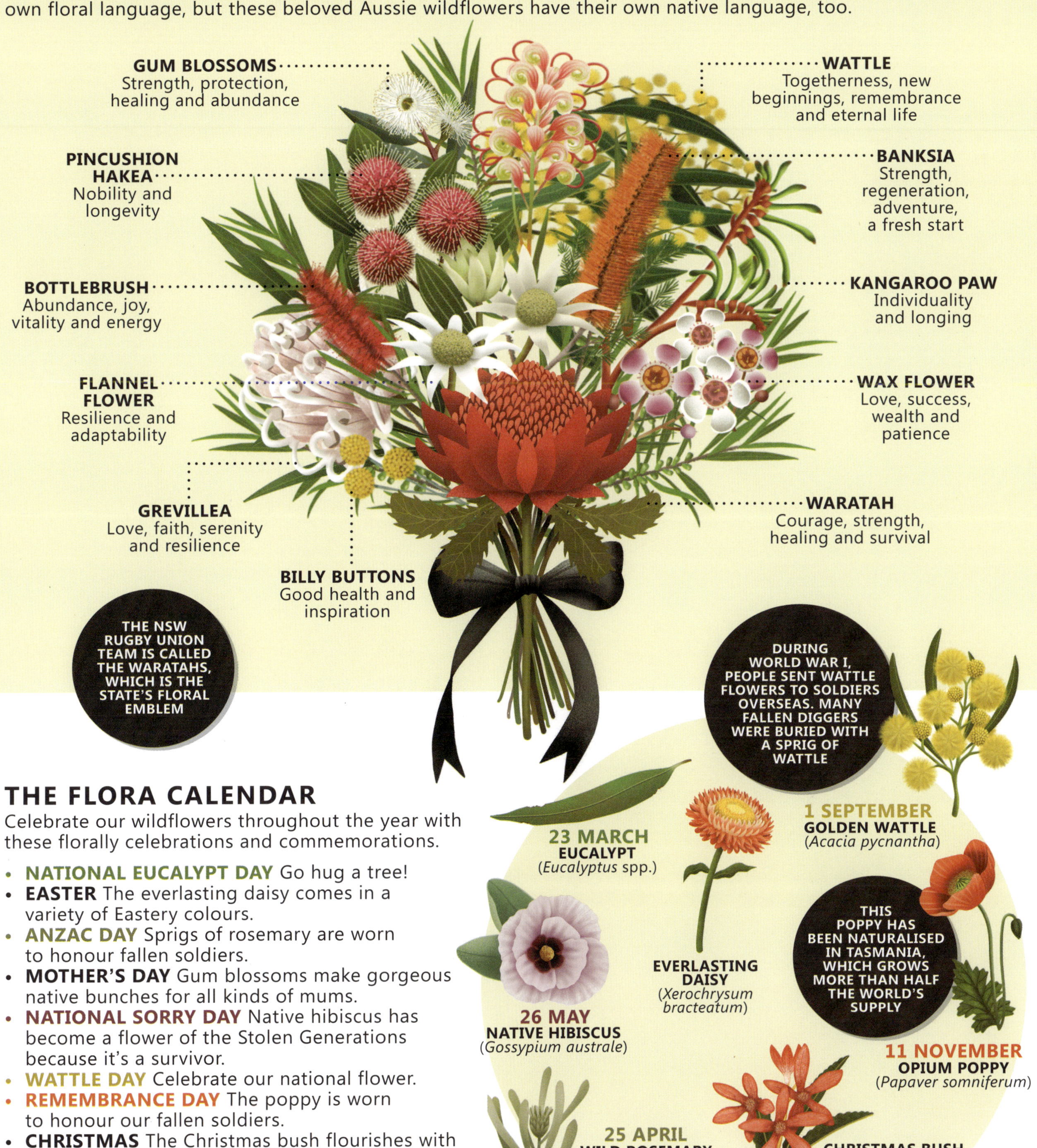

THE FLORA CALENDAR

Celebrate our wildflowers throughout the year with these florally celebrations and commemorations.

- **NATIONAL EUCALYPT DAY** Go hug a tree!
- **EASTER** The everlasting daisy comes in a variety of Eastery colours.
- **ANZAC DAY** Sprigs of rosemary are worn to honour fallen soldiers.
- **MOTHER'S DAY** Gum blossoms make gorgeous native bunches for all kinds of mums.
- **NATIONAL SORRY DAY** Native hibiscus has become a flower of the Stolen Generations because it's a survivor.
- **WATTLE DAY** Celebrate our national flower.
- **REMEMBRANCE DAY** The poppy is worn to honour our fallen soldiers.
- **CHRISTMAS** The Christmas bush flourishes with festive red blooms around mid to late December.

THE FUTURE

Australian plants are legendary survivors, yet over 1400 species are threatened, with 220 critically endangered. That's more than double the number of threatened animals. Our land has suffered terrible losses in biodiversity due to climate change, crop growing, habitat destruction, grazing animals like sheep and cattle, and the introduction of foreign plant species. What does the future hold for our beloved flora and what can we do about it?

AT RISK OF EXTINCTION

Losing species is a natural process, as plants (and animals) adapt and change through evolution. This normally takes many millions of years, but human effects on plants now take just a few decades. Global warming is the main villain, caused by high levels of carbon dioxide (CO_2) in the atmosphere.

GIANT KELP ALSO STORES HEAPS OF CARBON, YET 95 PER CENT OF TASMANIA'S KELP FORESTS HAVE BEEN LOST DUE TO CLIMATE CHANGE

CARBON WARRIORS

Plants are warriors when it comes to CO_2. They use it to make oxygen but they also store it, which keeps it out of the atmosphere. Mangrove forests cover just 0.1 per cent of Earth's surface, yet store 10 times more carbon than land forests! Unfortunately, one per cent of mangrove forest is lost each year and these VIP plants could completely disappear by 2100. Eucalypts like the Sydney blue gum also lift some pretty heavy carbon weight.

SYDNEY BLUE GUM
(*Eucalyptus saligna*)

PLANTS AT WORK

Plants work hard. They perform countless functions, but the most important job of all is the production of oxygen through photosynthesis. Without it, we'd have no ozone layer to protect us from the sun's harmful ultraviolet (UV) radiation. We'd have no fire and our water could become useless. And there would be no breathing, either—from the smallest single-celled bacteria through to insects and mammals like you!

PEOPLE AT WORK

Conservation groups, First Nations rangers, community groups, government agencies, scientists and researchers are working hard to save our flora, too. Long before European settlement, First Nations people used amazing techniques, like fire-stick farming, to beautifully manage our land. It's now vital to lean on their knowledge and expertise to protect and heal our flora.

THE FRUIT OF THE BLUE QUANDONG HAS IRIDESCENT BLUE SKIN THANKS TO A MICROSCOPIC STRUCTURE SIMILAR TO THAT FOUND IN BUTTERFLY WINGS

BLUE QUANDONG
(*Elaeocarpus grandis*)

HANDS OFF!

Some people like to pinch wild plants to sell or to add to their own collection, and the more rare and beautiful the plant, the better. The problem is that many plants don't survive cultivation. Just like our fauna, our flora thrives in a wild environment.

PERHAPS ONE TOO MANY NATIVE FOXGLOVES HAVE BEEN PICKED. THIS SPECIES IS NOW CRITICALLY ENDANGERED

NATIVE FOXGLOVE
(*Dasymalla axillaris*)

LEGENDARY RAINFORESTS

When Europeans arrived, just one per cent of Australia was covered by ancient rainforests. Today, three-quarters of those rainforests have been destroyed. The only remaining pockets are found on our east coast from far north Queensland down to Newcastle, and in the western half of Tasmania. The Wet Tropics World Heritage Area in far north Queensland is the second 'most irreplaceable' region on Earth. Precious trees like the blue quandong are already facing pressure due to habitat loss. Our forests really do need us more than ever.

CRITICALLY ENDANGERED PLANTS

Critically endangered means there is an extremely high risk of extinction in the immediate future. Here is a tiny slice of plants at risk, by state and territory.

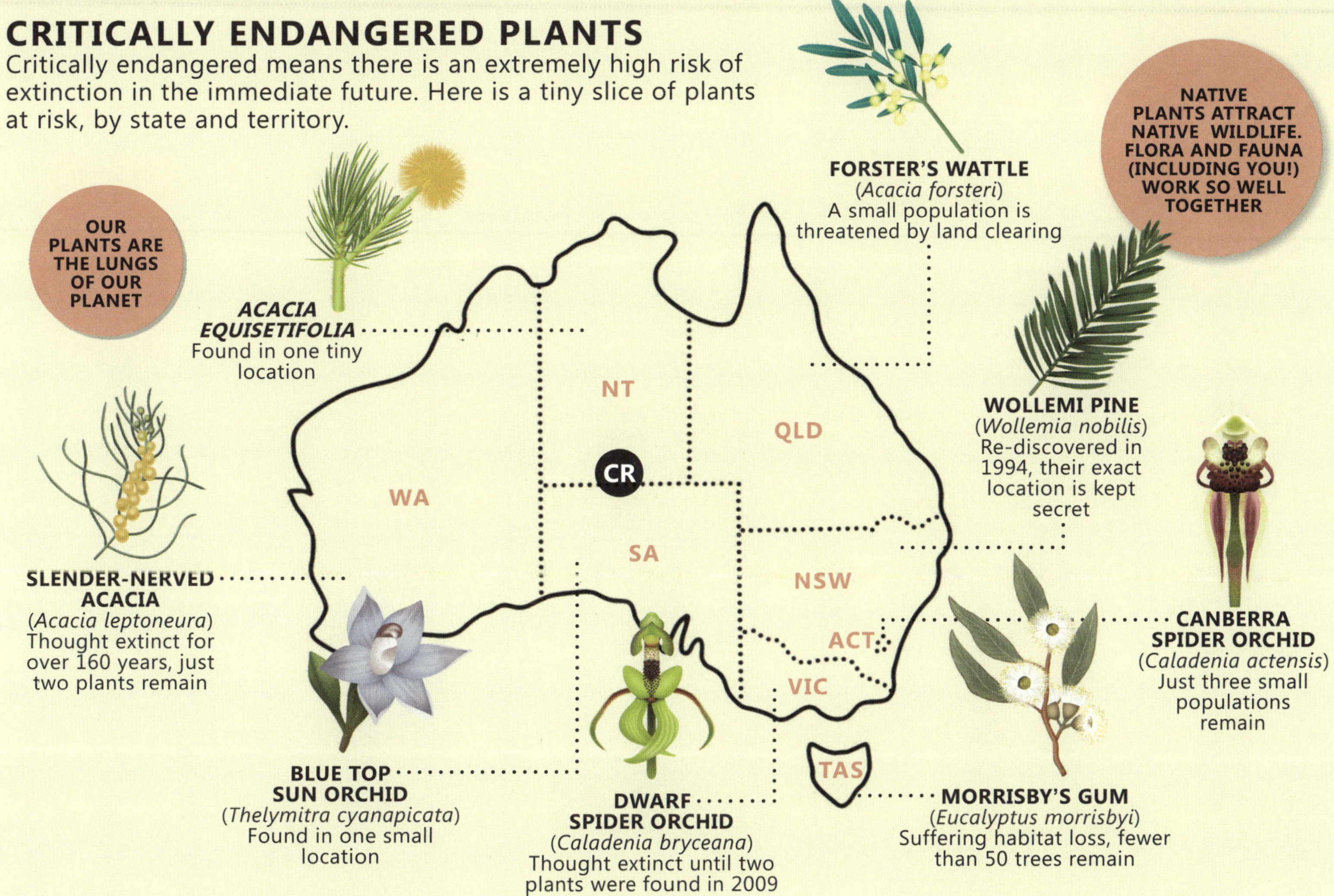

THE FUTURE IS BRIGHT

Just as you grow and change, our plants will continue to adapt to this ever-shifting world. Our ancient flora has beaten the odds and weathered some of the most challenging landscapes on Earth, so if any plants can survive, it's our little (and enormous!) Aussie battlers. Let's continue to explore, ask questions and share our love of nature. Like each tree in a forest, every act adds up ... and together, we can help our unique and rather curious native flora thrive for millions of years to come.

WHAT YOU CAN DO

- Plant your own **NATIVE SPECIES** or even a **BUSH FOOD GARDEN** at home or at school. Native plants rarely need fertilisers or pesticides, and need very little water.
- Try **TALKING TO YOUR PLANTS**! They may not speak your language but they do respond to sound vibrations, which improves photosynthesis and general health. Gentle singing works, too.
- Build an **INSECT HOTEL**. Our native bee populations are declining, and homemade insect hotels are a safe space for them to hatch their young. Search online for how to build the perfect little dwelling.
- It may sound weird—but **EAT MORE PLANTS**! Eating less meat has a positive effect on global warming.
- Learn about the ways local **FIRST NATIONS TRADITIONAL OWNERS** care for the land you live on.
- Join an **ENVIRONMENTAL ORGANISATION**, have a **FUNDRAISER** for environmental causes that affect our native flora, or organise a native **TREE PLANTING** at your school or local park.
- Write letters to your local council to organise a **CLEAN-UP DAY** or to suggest improvements to local ecosystems like parks and waterways.
- Protect our environment by reducing the things you **BUY AND USE**.
- Read and share books like **FLORA** to learn more about our incredible plants.

RE-USE, RECYCLE AND REPURPOSE AS MUCH AS YOU POSSIBLY CAN

OUR BACKYARD

For First Nations people, native plants were never unusual or curious. They were a way of life and health and ceremony for tens of thousands of years. When Europeans arrived in Australia, scientists, botanists and plant lovers marvelled at the strikingly beautiful 'new' species of flora, even though the ancestors of these plants were some of the most ancient on Earth. Over the years, artists have captured the splendour and unique nature of our native flora so we can document, learn and share each species for generations to come.

GRASS TREE
(*Xanthorrhoea spp.*)

GOLDEN WATTLE
(*Acacia pycnantha*)

RIVER RED GUM
(*Eucalyptus camaldulensis*)

WARATAH
(*Telopea speciosissima*)

STURT'S DESERT PEA
(Swainsona formosa)
RED AND GREEN KANGAROO PAW
(Anigozanthos manglesii)
BILLY BUTTONS
(Pycnosorus globosus)
SHOWY BANKSIA
(Banksia speciosa)

GLOSSARY

AERENCHYMA Spongy tissue in roots and stems that forms pockets of air.
AERIAL ROOTS Roots that grow upwards, into the air.
ALGAE Plant cousins that live in water and help keep the water healthy (single: ALGA).
ANCESTRY The evolutionary history of living things.
ANGIOSPERMS Flowering plants (they produce flowers, fruits and seeds).
ANTHER The top part of a stamen that makes and holds pollen.
ANTIBACTERIAL Substances that fight against bacteria to prevent infection.
ANTIOXIDANTS Compounds that protect cells from damage caused by unstable molecules (called free radicals).
AQUATIC Relating to or living in water.
ARIL An edible seed covering or attachment that attracts ants and other animals for seed dispersal.
AUTOGAMY Self-pollination—where a plant's flower is fertilised with its own pollen.
BACTERIA Microscopic, single-celled organisms that can be lovely or nasty!
BINOMIAL NAME Scientific name for each species, often written in Latin or Greek.
BIOCHEMICAL Relating to chemical processes and substances of living organisms.
BIODIVERSITY The variety of plant and animal life in particular habitats.
BRACT A modified leaf that sometimes forms flower-like structures.
BRYOPHYTES Non-vascular plants, including mosses, liverworts and hornworts.
BUTTRESS Above-ground roots that rise up and give stability to the tree trunk.
CALYX The outer part of a flower made up of sepals (usually green) and enclosing the petals.
CAUDEX A thickened, wood-like stem that may look like a trunk but is not.
CINEOLE A substance found in gum leaves that's toxic to most animals (but not koalas!).
CHLOROPHYLL The green pigment in plant cells that captures sunlight for photosynthesis.
CHLOROPLAST The solar-powered chlorophyll factories where photosynthesis takes place.
CLASSIFICATION Sorting plants into groups based on their similarities and differences.
CLONE Genetically identical plants that come from a single parent, often sprouting via the roots.
CLUSTERS Groups of flowers or fruits closely arranged on a stem.
CO-EVOLUTION Two or more species interacting and influencing each other's evolution over time.
COMPOUND LEAVES Leaves made up of many little leaflets.
COMPOUNDS Chemical substances that join together to make different elements.
CONES Reproductive forms in plants like conifers—the male cones produce pollen and females produce seeds.
CONSERVATION Protection and sustainable use of plants and their ecosystems.
CONVERGENT EVOLUTION Unrelated species evolving in remarkably similar ways, in different parts of the world.
COPPICING Cut tree stumps growing new shoots and eventually a new tree!
CORYMB A flat-topped cluster of flowers with stems of different lengths.
COTYLEDONS The baby leaves of a seedling, often the first leaves to appear after germination.
CULM The hollow stem of grasses or similar plants.
CULTIVATION The growing and caring of plants, either at home or for businesses like nurseries.
ENDEMIC Something that is found only in a specific area and nowhere else.
ENDOSPERM The part of a seed that provides nutrition to the developing plant embryo.
ENZYMES Proteins that cause or speed up chemical reactions in plants and animals.
EPICORMIC Buds that grow on a tree trunk, often after fire or pruning.
FIBROUS Made of fibres or thread-like material.
FILAMENTS Long, thin parts of a plant, like stamens.
FOLLICLES Dry fruits that split open to release seeds.
GALL An abnormal growth on a plant caused by insects or fungi.
GERMINATION When a seed starts developing into a plant.
GYMNOSPERMS Plants that produce seeds in cones or as spores (not inside fruit).

HALOPHYTIC Plants that have adapted to salty soils or coastal areas.
HAUSTORIA A special growth that attaches to other plants to steal their nutrients.
HELIOTROPISM When plants turn their leaves or flowers to face sunlight.
HERMAPHRODITIC Having both male and female reproductive organs in the same plant.
HORMONES Chemical messengers that help balance living organisms.
HYBRID A new variety—created by blending two or more species.
HYDROPHOBIC Repels water.
INFLORESCENCE A cluster of flowers on a single stem, often forming one larger 'flower'.
JUVENILE Young.
LAMINA The flat part of a leaf.
LAURASIA The ancient supercontinent that eventually split to form our northern hemisphere continents.
LIGNOTUBER A woody bulb at the base of some plants that helps it resprout.
MYCELIA The vegetative part of a fungus, consisting of a mass of thread-like structures.
MYCORRHIZAL FUNGI Fungi that form a relationship with plant roots and help with nutrient absorption.
NATURALISED A non-native species that has successfully established wild populations.
NEUROTOXIN A dangerous substance that can cause major damage to the body's nervous system.
NYCTINASTY The movement of plant parts in response to daily changes in light or temperature.
OPERCULUM A lid that can protect petals, stamens, spores or seeds.
ORGANISM A living thing.
OVARY/OVULE An ovary is where seeds develop and an ovule is a potential seed.
PARASITIC Plants that steal nutrients from other plants.
PARTHENOCARPIC Fruits that develop without fertilisation and are often seedless.
PEDUNCLE The stalk that supports a flower or fruit.
PETIOLE The stalk that connects a leaf to its stem.
PHLOEM A tube that transports sugars from the leaves to the rest of the plant.
PHYLLOCLADE A stem that resembles a leaf and can photosynthesise.
PHYLLODE A modified leaf that's not really a leaf but functions like a leaf! It's often flattened.
PHYTOPLANKTON Tiny plant-like organisms found in water.
PISTIL Female part of a flower that includes the stigma, style and ovary.
PNEUMATOPHORE A type of root that helps plants like mangroves get oxygen.
PROTISTA Single-celled organisms, like green algae, which is not a plant but is plant-like.
RHIZOME An underground stem that grows horizontally and produces new shoots and roots.
RIPARIAN Land that interacts with water, like the bank of a river or a lake's shore.
SCLEROPHYLL Plants with hard leaves that help prevent water loss.
SEPAL Modified leaves (often green) that surround a bud then go on to form the base of a flower.
SEROTINY When plants release seeds in response to things like fire, drought, flood or the seasons.
SESSILE Leaves that are attached to a branch without any leaf stalk.
SPORES Teensy reproductive cells that grow into plants.
STAMEN The male part of a flower, which produces pollen.
STIGMA Found at the top of a flower's style, the stigma receives pollen.
STYLE A flower's long, thin tube that connects the stigma to the ovary.
THERMOREGULATE A plant adjusting its own temperature.
THIGMONASTY When a plant moves in response to touch.
TUBER A swollen, underground storage unit, like a potato.
VASCULAR Plants with tubes that transport water and sugars.
XYLEM A tube that transports water and nutrients from the roots to the rest of the plant.

INDEX

FOR SUSAN. THANK YOU. —TM x

THANK YOU

A forest full of thanks to Lauren Smith, Amelia Hartney, Kath Kovac, Tricia Fitzgerald, Madeleine Warburton and to the dedicated people who make conservation their life's work (I'm certain they have chlorophyll in their veins). Love and thanks to Irma Gold, Dee White and my family, for all their support. And thanks to artsACT for the grant that made this book possible.

Published by National Library of Australia Publishing
Canberra ACT 2600

ISBN: 9781922507716

First published 2024, reprinted 2024, twice in 2025

The National Library of Australia acknowledges Australia's First Nations Peoples—the First Australians—as the Traditional Owners and Custodians of this land and gives respect to the Elders—past and present—and through them to all Australian Aboriginal and Torres Strait Islander people.

Publisher: Lauren Smith
Managing editor: Amelia Hartney
Editors: Kath Kovac and Tricia Fitzgerald
Designer: Tania McCartney
Image coordinator: Madeleine Warburton
Printed in China through Asia Pacific Offset on FSC®-certified paper

Find out more about NLA Publishing at library.gov.au/discover/nla-publishing

A catalogue record for this book is available from the National Library of Australia.

Supported by:

FIRST NATIONS THANK YOU

Tania McCartney and the National Library of Australia would like to thank C.J. Fisher of the Kuku Yalanji people, Beverley Hand of the Gubbi Gubbi people, Clinton Walker of the Ngarluma people, Gail Yorkshire, Lynette Knapp and Vanessa Martin of the Noongar–Wudjari people, Shaeleigh Swan of the Aṉangu people and Michael Lyons of the Wiradjuri people for sharing their knowledge and stories with us. Thanks, also, to Nicole Kilby of The Healing Foundation, Denise Smith-Ali of the Noongar Boodjar Language Cultural Aboriginal Corporation and Nat Raisbeck-Brown, coordinator of CSIRO's Australian Living Atlas.

IMAGE COLLECTION

- **GRASS TREE** Percy Clarke, Grass Tree (*Xanthorrhoea*), c.1886, nla.cat-vn1403492
- **GOLDEN WATTLE** Ellis Rowan, *Acacia pycnantha*, c.1880s, nla.cat-vn2841608
- **RIVER RED GUM** Ellis Rowan, *Eucalyptus camaldulensis*, c.1880s, nla.cat-vn2845187
- **WARATAH** Adam Forster, *Telopea speciosissima*, 1916, nla.cat-vn717250
- **STURT'S DESERT PEA** Marrianne Collinson Campbell, Sturts Desert Pea, c.1800s, nla.cat-vn3624304
- **RED AND GREEN KANGAROO PAW** Ellis Rowan, *Anigozanthos manglesii*, c.1880s, nla.cat-vn1338508
- **BILLY BUTTONS** Ellis Rowan, *Pycnosorus globosus*, c.1880s, nla.cat-vn2848799
- **SHOWY BANKSIA** Ferdinand Bauer, *Banksia speciosa*, 1995, nla.cat-vn2288485